CHERRY STONES

Lifelong friends Sophie Wheeler and Kate Kent have reached a crisis in their love lives. James Simpson has proposed to Sophie, but what exactly are his motives? Is he too self-centred to marry? Kate's partner is Mark Roberts, but all the passion seems gone from their relationship. However, Kate is involved in a campaign to save Rosebank, a retirement home, from being sold to a supermarket chain. Will Mark's offer to help the group bring them closer together?

CATRIONA McCUAIG

CHERRY STONES

Complete and Unabridged

LINFORD
Leicester

First published in Great Britain in 2008

First Linford Edition
published 2009

British Library CIP Data

McCuaig, Catriona.
    Cherry stones - - (Linford romance library)
    1. Love stories.
    2. Large type books.
    I. Title II. Series
    823.9'2–dc22

    ISBN 978–1–84782–794–4

1

James had certainly made an effort; Sophie had to give him that at least. The restaurant he'd chosen was a new one, very smart; down by the river, a far cry from the fast food outlets where they usually grazed. This one had real tablecloths, with napkins to match; and it was a relief to have real silverware to work with, rather than the usual struggle to cut up the food with fiddly plastic knives and forks.

Madden's had subdued lighting, soft music and attentive waiters, and there were real flowers on the table. Sweet peas, Sophie's favourite, but that was probably coincidence. James surely couldn't have arranged that. Yes, he'd obviously gone to some lengths to create the right atmosphere for what he was about to say, but then, why shouldn't he?

It was Sophie who made all the running during their four years together, shivering on the sidelines at football games, going with him to jazz concerts when she much preferred show tunes, and turning up at his office parties, where everyone knew each other, talked shop and ignored her.

Now for the big moment! James waved away the waiter, took her hands in his, and gazed earnestly into her blue eyes. 'Shall we get married, Soph?'

She waited expectantly. This was no time to remind him that she hated being called Soph. Even more, she hated the stupid remark he always made when they met new people, something about him always being comfortable when he was with her, 'like an old sofa, haw, haw!' Obviously he wasn't about to get down on one knee, not in full view of the other diners, but she'd hoped for something a little more romantic than this! Perhaps a declaration of love before he reached into an inside pocket and brought out a certain little velvet-lined box?

'Well?' he demanded. 'Don't you have something to say? Surely you're not going to come over all Victorian on me? 'This is so sudden, Sir,' and all that stuff!'

Sophie swallowed hard. 'It's a bit of a surprise, that's all. And I do need time to think, James. This is the most important decision of my life and I don't want to get it wrong.'

'All right, but don't take too long making up your mind, will you? If I'm going to get married at all, this is the perfect time for it. I haven't got around to telling you this before, but I'm afraid I'm being made redundant. Downsizing, they call it, but it all amounts to the same thing. I've seen it coming ever since Fraser & Dickens merged with Burgess & Co.; there's too much duplication of staff. I'm not the only one, of course. Williams and Todd are leaving, too. We found out yesterday.'

'I'm so sorry, James! I had no idea.' Sophie was shocked. She had always understood that the public relations world was a cutthroat sort of business, but she hadn't realised that his job was at stake. 'What on earth will you do now?'

He picked up the salt shaker, absentmindedly shaking a few grains on to his empty plate. 'That's the whole point, don't you see? I'll be getting a pretty decent golden handshake, so here's my chance to write that novel I've always talked about. But for this I might never have got down to it.'

She frowned. 'But surely this is no time to be getting married, then? I don't mean to be a wet blanket, but isn't it awfully hard to break into the world of book publishing? Some people seem to attempt it for years without getting anywhere.'

'As I see it, the timing couldn't be better! I'll give up my flat when we get married and move into your place. Two can live as cheaply as one, and all that. I'll have my redundancy money, and you'll still be working, of course. And we'll be even better off when you get that promotion you're expecting.'

Sophie was relieved when they were interrupted by the waiter, wanting to know if they'd care to see the dessert trolley. James was about to refuse, but she quickly said that she'd love something rich and creamy, even though she didn't feel in the least bit interested. She needed to defuse the situation before she lost her temper.

'I am flattered, James,' she murmured, when the man had moved away, 'and I will let you know, very soon. I must discuss this with Mum first.' This was a rather lame excuse but all she could think of on the spur of the moment.

'Well, all right,' he grumbled, 'but I don't see why! You've hinted at it often enough. Surely your husband-to-be should be the first to know when you're getting married, not your mother!'

The rest of the meal was eaten in silence, with Sophie trying to swallow the gateau which tasted like sawdust in her mouth, and James stirring his coffee unnecessarily hard.

He was rather cool when he left her outside her flat at the end of the evening, and when she invited him in for coffee he refused, saying that he'd already had more than enough at the restaurant. Sophie had barely shut the door on him before she was on the phone to her best friend, Kate.

'I do hope you weren't already in bed, or asleep, or something? Look, I know it's awfully late, but I'm bursting to talk to you. Could I possibly pop round now?'

'Of course. Mark is out and I was just sitting here trying to work out a new knitting pattern.'

Without bothering to change, Sophie flew round to her friend's flat, which luckily was only a few minutes' walk from her own.

'My goodness, you're dressed to kill, aren't you? Been somewhere nice, then?' Kate smiled.

'*Madden's.*'

'I say! That's pushing the boat out a bit! It must have been a special occasion, by the sound of it! I haven't forgotten your birthday, have I?'

Sophie raised both hands dramatically. 'James proposed!'

'No. Oh, that's wonderful! Congratulations!' Kate leaned forward to hug her friend, but Sophie fended her off.

'It's a bit early for that. I haven't given him an answer yet.'

Kate sat down again. 'I don't get it. You've been moaning for ages about his lack of commitment, so what's the problem now? If I were you I'd snap him up before he changes his mind.'

'Oh, Kate! I thought I'd be over the moon when he finally did come to the point, and now I feel sort of flat. The atmosphere was perfect — the music, soft lights and all that — but somehow it was all a big let-down. He didn't say anything about being head over heels in love, or not wanting to live without me. Not the sort of things a girl dreams about.'

'You've been reading too many magazine stories, Sophie. Most men aren't like that. I'm sure he does love you; he just can't find the words to express his true feelings.'

'I can't help feeling that this is meant to be a marriage of convenience, Kate. That's what it sounded like to me.'

Kate burst out laughing. 'A marriage of convenience! Now I know you've been reading historical novels.'

'Oh, not that sort of convenience,' Despite her agitation Sophie smiled. 'No. He's lost his job, and he wants to move into my flat and write the great British novel, while I keep right on working at the bank. I have the feeling that I'm being used, Kate.'

Kate picked up her knitting, grimaced, and put it down again. 'I'm sorry he's been made redundant, but aren't you making too much of this? You wouldn't keep on two flats after the wedding in any case, and don't you mean to keep working anyway? Most women do nowadays, at least until the children come along, and being Assistant Manager is something you've worked hard for. Why would you want to give that up?'

Sophie shrugged. 'I don't. It's just that he's always managed to avoid commitment until now and suddenly, when it suits him to combine our resources, he's hearing wedding bells. What about me, then? Doesn't it matter what I want?'

'At least he's asked you to marry him, Sophie. He could have suggested you just move in together.'

'Ah, but that wouldn't be good enough for James Simpson! Where's the security in that? I could walk out at any time if I got fed up, you see.'

They were going round in circles now. Kate listened, making all the right noises, but she couldn't help thinking about her own situation with her partner, Mark. They'd been together for over a year now, which was commitment of a sort, but he still didn't seem ready to settle down permanently. In the beginning he'd suggested they move in together 'and see how we get on' but now he seemed content to let the situation drag on forever.

Meanwhile, Kate longed to start a family, but she was old fashioned enough to think she should be married first.

'Are you listening to me?' Sophie demanded, when no response was forthcoming to her latest question.

'What? Oh, sorry! My mind was wandering. It's getting a bit late, that's all, and Mark isn't back yet. Where on earth can he have got to?'

Sophie stood up, yawning. 'Yes, I really should be going, though I'm sure I'll never get to sleep tonight. It wouldn't do to be late for work in the morning. Got to make a good impression if I'm to get that promotion to Branch Manager.'

'Yes, well, good luck with that, and I hope you get things sorted out in your mind soon.'

'If I do decide to go through with it,

why don't we make it a double wedding?'

'What, you mean me and Mark?'

'Fool! Of course you and Mark! How many men do you have on your string, anyway? Seriously, though, I'd love it if we did that; I can see it now, two brides coming down the aisle together. I wonder how that works? Do they saunter down side by side, or one behind the other?'

'Go home!' Kate laughed, pushing her friend out of the door. As the sound of Sophie's footsteps receded down the hall, Kate let out a long breath. She hadn't wanted to rain on her friend's parade, as her American cousin would have put it, but things were far from being all right between herself and Mark. They had settled into a routine where she did ninety per cent of the cooking and cleaning while he came and went as he pleased. She wanted to be more than a live-in housemaid.

Action was clearly called for. It was far too late to say anything tonight, of course: he'd be tired when he finally came in, but some day soon she'd have it out with him. She'd start by giving him Sophie's news, and see where that led.

2

Joan wheeler looked at her daughter in delight. 'At last! After four years I was beginning to think he'd never pop the question! Where's the ring, then? Let's have a look!' She reached for Sophie's left hand, tutting her disappointment when she took in the fact that the third finger was bare of any adornment.

'Steady on, Mum! I haven't accepted him yet.'

'It's a foregone conclusion, though, isn't it? What's the matter, love? Not having second thoughts, are you?'

'Perhaps I am. I was expecting to be swept off my feet if this day ever did arrive, but now it all seems so, well, clinical, somehow. James has it all down pat and I'm just supposed to fall in with his plans, when it suits him. I don't want my wedding to be a hole in the corner sort of affair, Mum.

'It doesn't have to be a big do, but I've always dreamed of turning up at the church on Dad's arm, all dressed in white, with cousin Angela's sweet little twins as bridesmaids. I won't be rushed into anything just because James has been made redundant.'

'Of course not, dear. Planning a wedding takes time. Next June would be nice, or what about a lovely Christmas one, with the church decorated with holly?'

'Mum, listen to me, please! I came to you hoping you'd help me decide what to do. Should I accept James, or not?'

Joan became serious at once. 'Only you know that, dear; I can't decide that for you, and furthermore I shouldn't even try. And if you do have doubts, perhaps that's a sign that you shouldn't go through with it. This is an important step in your life. Better to suffer the pain of a break up now than make a mistake you'll regret later.

'As I see it, the thing to do is to discuss all this with James. Be honest and tell him exactly how this has made you feel.'

'Mum! I couldn't.'

'You can, and you will, my girl. It's one thing for a man to be a bit masterful, as they used to say in my day, but if he won't let you have your say, that isn't a good sign. Marriage is a matter of give and take, or it should be.'

'He won't like it.'

'That's what I mean.' Joan began to talk about something else then, refusing to let Sophie return to the subject of James Simpson. When her daughter had left the house, grumbling, she went in search of her husband and poured out her thoughts to him.

'Doesn't sound like much of a prospect to me,' he grunted, turning over the pages of his newspaper and only half listening. 'If I had my way she'd kick the chap into touch. He's kept her hanging about far too long, if you ask me.'

'I am asking you, love! Should I have

spoken out and told her that, do you think?'

'Would it have made any difference if you had? Girls don't listen to their parents nowadays; you should know that by now.'

Joan longed to rush over to see James and pin him back by the ears. Tell him exactly what she thought of him, and insist he treat her daughter properly, or else! Of course, she could do no such thing, and that was so hard. It was true what people said; you never stopped being a mother, even when your children were grown up!

★　★　★

'James, we have to talk.'

Sophie had let three days elapse since that historic moment at *Madden's* restaurant, and now she felt that the time had come to sort things out. She stopped at the bakery on the way to his flat and chose several pastries, hoping that the gift would sweeten him up. He had once joked that he'd do anything to get his hands on an Eccles cake.

'What's in that bag?' he greeted her. 'I hope it's something nice to go with the coffee I've just brewed.'

'Did you hear what I said?'

'Of course I did. Not deaf, am I? I hope you've come to tell me you've made up your mind at last.'

She ignored that remark. They were beginning to sound like an old married couple, bickering away, not at all like two people in love, who were planning the wedding of their dreams. Well, her dreams, she amended.

'Of course I want to marry you, James,' she murmured, surprising herself. She hadn't known until that moment that she was actually going to accept his proposal. 'As I told you, I wanted to discuss this at home, to see what might do for a wedding date. Mum suggests that June would be ideal.'

'June?' he squeaked. 'Next June?'

'Well, it's July now, so it could hardly

17

be June of this year, could it?'

'But that's so far off, Soph!'

'We could consider Christmas, I suppose, but that would be a bit of a rush. There's so much to plan.'

He groaned. 'Do we really have to go through all that business of morning dress, and wedding cakes and whatnot? Why not just nip down to the registrar's office and get it over with?'

Really, this was too bad! Where was the excitement and the joy of looking forward to their future life together? Where was the romance?

'Getting married is important to me,' she said firmly. 'I don't want a shabby little do in some back street office. I want all our friends and relations around me when we tie the knot. It doesn't have to cost a lot of money but it has to mean something. I want to be able to look back on it in years to come, and remember how lovely it all was.'

'You want! You want! Is that all you can say? What about what I want, hey? Don't you care about that?'

'Of course I do, James. Come on, have your say.'

'Have you forgotten what I told you, Sophie? I've been made redundant. I mean to take this opportunity to write my novel. I've always known I could do it, if only I had the time, and this seems like the perfect moment.'

'I see that. But as you said, you'll have your redundancy money. You can live on that while you do your writing.'

He stuck out his lower lip, looking for all the world like a small boy whose sand castle has just been ruined by a giant wave. 'Yes, and have it all swallowed up paying rent and all the rest. What a waste that would be, especially when there's plenty of room in your flat. I thought we could convert that little sewing room of yours into an office for me, somewhere to retire to and shut the door when I was working.'

Sophie Wheeler was not the sort of person who threw tantrums or flew into sudden rages, but now she felt a surge of anger welling up inside her. Clenching her fists inside the pockets of her jeans she struggled for control before allowing herself to respond to that little remark.

'I thought I could give up my flat and come to you,' she improvised. 'It's much closer to the bank and I wouldn't have so far to travel to work from there. We could share the rent, if that's what's bothering you.'

His mouth opened but no words came out. 'Let's hear what you've got to say to that, James Simpson!' Sophie thought.

'Yes, well, it's something to think about,' he said at last, but it was quite obvious that he didn't like her idea at all. Neither did she, actually. Her preference was for them to give up both flats, and start somewhere new together. They probably couldn't afford to buy a house right now, but they could start saving for a deposit. She mentioned this to James.

'No need for that, Soph. When I sell

my book we'll be able to buy our dream house, cash down. Just you wait and see.'

She wanted to say 'pigs might fly' but that would be far too cruel and unnecessary. Instead, she suggested that he might look for another job, and do his writing in his spare time, thus hedging his bets. He looked at her as if she'd made some obscene suggestion.

'Really, Sophie, don't you have any faith in me at all?'

'Yes, James, I do, but surely writing a book can't be as easy as all that? Have you ever written anything before, apart from reports at work, of course?'

'My essays were highly praised at university,' he said stiffly. 'But this is hardly the point, is it? We're supposed to be discussing our marriage, but now I'm beginning to wonder if it was such a good idea after all. A wife is supposed to support her husband, and it seems to me as if you're not going to be very good at that!'

This was fast deteriorating into an

out and out brawl. Time to nip it in the bud, Sophie decided. 'We'll talk again when you're in a better mood,' she told him, picking up her handbag and preparing to go. Somehow she managed to keep from slamming the door behind her.

Honestly, the man's ideas were about a hundred years out of date! If he behaved like this now, what on earth would he be like when they'd been married for a few years? Perhaps her mother was right and it was best to call it a day. Unfortunately, for all his faults, Sophie still loved James, and what was she going to do about that?

3

Kate had met Mark Roberts two years earlier, at a party. Now, looking back, she shuddered to think of how close they had come to not meeting at all. She'd been looking forward to the evening but at the last minute had almost decided not to go. It was a wild, wet night, and she could feel a cold coming on. It was tempting to stay indoors and go to bed early, with the new Maeve Binchy. One good thing about being a librarian was that she could have first pick of the new arrivals!

It was only the prospect of letting Sophie down that changed her mind. She pulled herself together and decided that she simply must turn up. Sophie was giving the party for her boyfriend, James Simpson, and several of his friends from work would be there.

Sophie was in a flat spin wondering

how she could hold it all together. It wasn't the sort of event where you turned up clutching a bottle of plonk and danced to loud music. There was to be a sit-down meal, with the food cooked by Sophie herself in the hope of impressing James. Kate had promised to be there to lend support.

Having missed one bus, she arrived when the party was in full swing.

'Where have you been?' Sophie hissed. 'I thought you weren't coming!'

'Why? I'm not that late, am I? Nobody turns up on time for parties, anyway.'

'I want you to circulate. I've got to keep an eye on things in the kitchen. I can't do everything myself.'

'Can't James circulate?' Out of the corner of her eye Kate could see the handsome James across the room, holding forth to several giggling females. The men were standing about in clumps, apparently ignoring the spectacle.

'See that man over there? Go and talk to him,' Sophie ordered. 'He's been standing there for ages, staring out of the window, although I can't imagine what he's looking at. There's nothing to see out there, even in daylight, which it isn't now, of course.'

Katie knew that when Sophie started to ramble on like this, the next stage was hysteria, so she smiled and went over to the solitary figure, wishing she had some cheeky chat-up line to startle him with. As it happened, he spoke first.

'Thank goodness! I thought I was being shunned completely. Can you talk, or are you just here for decoration? I must say you look absolutely stunning in that dress! What do they call that colour? Scarlet, is it?'

'Er, flame, I think,' Kate stammered, turning almost as red as her floaty dress. 'And surely you have lots of people to talk to? Aren't all these people form work?'

'Oh, I don't work with James. He only asked me to come along because he's been to one or two bashes of mine.

25

Our flats are in the same building, you see. I'm Mark Roberts, by the way.'

'Kate Kent. So you're not in the public relations business, then.'

'Heaven forbid! No, I'm a nurse. And what about you?'

Somehow they drifted into a corner and were soon exchanging notes about their lives. They kept saying how amazing it was that they had so much in common. For one thing, both were tired of having to explain their career choices to other people.

'A nurse. How funny! That's the usual reaction,' Mark explained. 'Believe it or not, there are still some people who think that men are always doctors and women are nurses, and not the other way around. Usually the next insulting comment is that they suppose I'm a nurse because I didn't have the brains to become a doctor! My grades weren't good enough to get me into med school, as it happens, but that never was my aim in the first place. I wanted the hands-on job of actually helping people to heal, and that's what nursing is.'

Kate smiled. She knew she should be helping Sophie to sort out the kitchen, but she was intrigued by this earnest man. She couldn't decide whether he was being defensive or simply being enthusiastic about his work. Perhaps a bit of both.

She found herself looking at his eyes, which were just the right sort of colour to go with his reddish hair. Were they brown, or more green than anything? Hazel was probably the correct term. He wasn't handsome, exactly — not like James Simpson, who was too dishy for his own good — but he was certainly appealing in an out-doorsy sort of way. She concluded that he probably played rugger or something on his weekends off.

'Hello! Earth to Kate!'

'Oh, sorry!' she blushed. 'I was thinking about um . . .'

'Was I boring you? I do tend to get carried away sometimes. Just think yourself lucky I didn't regale you with all the gory details of the seamier side of the job! It's your turn now. What are you? A fashion model? An up-and-coming movie starlet?'

'I'm a librarian.'

'A librarian! You don't look a bit like one!'

Kate laughed. 'Now who's falling back on stereotypes? There's more to being a librarian than stamping books, you know, especially with all the modern technology we have to deal with.' She paused for a moment, thinking about all the computers they had at work, some used for the day-to-day operation of the library, and others, which gave patrons access to the Internet.

'Touché! It's just that I remember the old girl who was in charge of my library when I was a kid. Horn-rimmed spectacles, grey hair in a bun, droopy hemlines and sensible shoes, not to mention a voice like a fog horn to shush anyone who spoke above a whisper!'

28

They grinned at each other, not quite knowing why.

The evening passed like a dream. Kate was sure that Mark was going to ask her out, but it didn't happen. She toyed with the idea of asking him, it was the twenty-first century, after all, but she was afraid of making a fool of herself. For all she knew he already had a steady girlfriend. In a hospital the size of Branksome General he could have his pick of women who shared his views of life, and she could do without being told 'thanks, but no thanks' if he wasn't interested.

Therefore she was surprised to look up from her desk several mornings later, to find Mark standing in front of her, holding a bunch of colourful daisies, which he thrust under her nose. 'Here, these are for you!'

'How pretty! Did you remove them from some poor patient's bedside?'

'Of course not. I nicked them from the cemetery on my way here.'

They grinned at each other, oblivious

to the shocked stare of an elderly woman who was waiting for Kate's attention.

'How do I send this e-mail to my niece in Australia?' she demanded at last, when it looked as if the pair would remain frozen to the spot forever. She waved a crumpled sheet of paper under Kate's nose. 'Our Dorothy says you can put this into one of them computers and somehow it comes out the other end. I don't believe a word of it myself, but she swears it's true.'

'I can't talk now,' Kate told Mark, 'but if you can come back in about fifteen minutes I'm due for my coffee break then. OK?'

He nodded and walked away in the direction of the magazine racks, hearing Kate's patient voice as she dealt with the bewildered woman. 'Is it a fax you wanted to send, Miss Brown? Does your niece have a fax machine?'

'I don't know, I'm sure. Our Dorothy didn't say.'

'Only if it's an e-mail you want to

send, you'll need to type this into the computer.'

'Oh, I couldn't do that!'

'Don't worry, I'll help you. There's nothing to it, really.'

Mark smiled to himself. There didn't seem to be much difference between their two jobs. Both were about helping people. He had to deal with many elderly people like Miss Brown, all of them anxious about dealing with a world which was becoming increasingly difficult for them to understand.

As he waited for Kate to become free, an idea crystallised in his mind. Some day he would like to specialise in geriatric nursing. There was so much that needed to be done in that field, and on top of that, anyone who went into that sort of work would never be out of a job. He would look into that before very much longer.

After that day, Kate and Mark quickly became an item. Within six months he had suggested that they move in together, and she quickly

31

agreed. It all seemed so right. Sophie, when Kate told her the news, was a bit miffed.

'I've been going out with James for two years, and he's never asked me to live with him. I've hinted and hinted but he always says it's not the right time. There's always some excuse.'

'He's not seeing anyone else, is he?'

'No, nothing like that. He's just afraid of commitment. You are lucky, Kate.'

Kate dragged her mind back to the present. James had kept dragging his heels until now, after dating Sophie for four years, he'd finally popped the question. It was just too bad that the poor girl was now having doubts about whether she wanted to spend the rest of her life catering to his whims and moods.

As for Kate and Mark, they'd been partners for two years, and hardly ever had a cross word, which was good. So why, then, was she also beginning to feel that the grass might be greener on the other side of the fence?

'We haven't come to join the library,' the taller of the two women was explaining to Kate's assistant, Miriam. 'We don't have time for reading.' The tone of her voice seemed to indicate that settling down with a good book was some kind of character defect. Her companion nodded in agreement.

Well, different strokes for different folks, Kate thought. Modern libraries had many things to offer besides books, including magazines, videos, CDs and access to the Internet. Their branch occasionally put on seminars and workshops, on a variety of subjects.

'Can I help?' she asked, seeing that Miriam was floundering.

'Are you the head librarian?'

'Yes, I am. Did you need something in particular?'

'It's Rosebank!' the short woman was still nodding. Either she was extremely agitated or she had some sort of medical condition, Kate decided.

'Rosebank?'

'Yes, yes, the old folks' home!'

'The senior citizens' retirement home,' the friend corrected reprovingly. 'It's about to close and something has to be done about it.'

Kate knew about the privately run facility, of course. On occasions when a resident fancied a book which was not kept in the small library there, the matron asked to have a copy sent out on loan. Kate herself had sometimes been the one to make the delivery.

Rosebank, which had long ago been a private home, was a beautiful old house, set in lovely grounds. Hardly a stately home, but certainly top drawer. It would indeed be a shame if the place had to close.

'We could find out about grants and so on,' she murmured, 'and if you're putting on a fund raising drive you're welcome to display a poster here. Other than that, I'm not sure what more we can do. Perhaps you can get The Gazette to run a story about the problem?'

'I told you this wouldn't work, Phyllis!' the nodding woman wailed. 'Poor Aunt Gertie! I'll just have to take her to live with me, and how I'll manage I just don't know! We never did get on, and she's more cranky than ever in her old age!'

'Nonsense, Millie! As I said, the library is as good a place as any to start. They're supposed to be running a public service here, aren't they?' She stared at Kate accusingly.

Katie quailed. 'What would you like me to do, Mrs . . . ?'

'Seabourne. To start with, I'd like you to host a public meeting here, to discuss the situation. We thought about having it in the town hall, but this is a much better venue. You can talk it up to your patrons when they come in to change their books. Make them understand how vital this is.'

Kate wasn't sure how it happened, but somehow she'd let herself be talked into chairing a meeting to discuss the issue, and providing tea and biscuits into the bargain!

Of course, it was in a good cause. Where would the residents go if Rosebank were to be closed? The local state facilities were filled to overflowing, and besides, they probably thought of the place as their home. It would be too bad if they had to leave those pleasant surroundings.

Mark was enthusiastic when he heard about the coming meeting.

'Good on yer, Katie! I'll come along and support you, of course. Someone has to take up the cudgels for these people, who can't fight for themselves. I know how stressed out some of our older patients are when it's time for them to be discharged, with nowhere to go. I'm proud of you for taking a stand!'

He beamed approvingly, and she didn't have the heart to explain that she wasn't all that keen to get involved. She believed that something should be done, of course she did, but she had her own pet causes and she didn't want to spread herself too thinly. Still, Mark seemed pleased with her, so why not strike while the iron was hot?

'Did I mention that Sophie is getting engaged?' she began.

'Only about a dozen times! I suppose she wants you to be a bridesmaid when the happy day arrives?'

'Not exactly. In fact, she wondered if we'd like to make it a double wedding.' She held her breath, waiting.

'A double wedding!' he frowned. 'With you and me, do you mean?'

'I suppose so. Yes, why not?'

A cloud seemed to have come over the sun, if his expression was anything to go by. Just when Kate was beginning to think that he wasn't going to respond, Mark grasped her hand, looked into her eyes and then looked away again. He seemed to be struggling to find the right words.

'Kate — love — when have I ever said anything about marriage?'

'What?' confused, she pulled her hand away.

'You can't pin this one on me. I've

never mentioned the subject, have I?'

'Well, no, but I thought it was the logical way to go. We've been living together for ages and I assumed that eventually we'd tie the knot. Isn't that what people do?'

'Look, I didn't want to have to say this, but you've forced me to it. You mustn't take this personally, but I don't want to marry you.'

'You don't want to marry me!'

'I'm afraid not.'

'But why, Mark? Is there someone else? Is that it?'

He shook his head.

'Then what is it? We love each other, don't we? Don't you love me, Mark?'

He was avoiding her eye now. 'You know I do. Marriage is a big step, though, Kate. Some day, when I meet the girl I want to spend the rest of my life with, then I'll consider it. Until then, it's not for me.'

Kate pressed her hands against the sudden pain in her chest. She hoped she wasn't having a heart attack. She took a few deep breaths and felt her pulse rate slow down.

'So let me get this straight. You're saying I'll do for now, until something better comes along. Is that it, Mark?'

'Aw, I wouldn't put it like that,' he muttered. 'Look, I think I'll wander down to the pub for a bit. Give you time to calm down.'

'Don't you dare walk out on me, Mark Roberts!' she yelped. But she was talking to thin air. She rushed over to discuss this turn of events with Sophie. It was her friend's turn to provide a shoulder to cry on.

'The brute!' Sophie snapped, when she'd heard what Kate had to say. 'I'd walk out, if I were you. You can stay here for a bit, until you get yourself sorted. If you want, I'll come over to your place right now and help you pack your things. What he needs is a short, sharp shock! It will serve him right to come home and find you've left him.'

'But I don't want to leave, Sophie! As long as Mark wants me to stay, we have a chance of working things out. When he stops to realise how much I do for him, he may have second thoughts.'

'Oh, I've no doubt he'll want you to stay,' Sophie scoffed. 'He couldn't have a more comfortable billet if he was still living at home with mum! He gets all his washing and ironing done, and you do the lion's share of the cooking and cleaning as well.'

'You're not telling me anything I don't already know.'

4

The Day of Reckoning is Nigh! Sophie smiled as she glanced up at the slogan on the billboard. Was that from the Bible? It was meant as some sort of religious message, anyway. Her day of reckoning was coming closer, and she couldn't wait for that glorious moment when her appointment as Branch Manager was confirmed.

She'd worked so hard to achieve that pinnacle and, once the job was safely in her pocket, with its improvement in salary, she'd be able to think about her future. Our future, she corrected herself, because she still meant to marry James, although not on his terms alone.

It had always been inevitable that she'd get a job in banking. Even as a little girl in elementary school she'd been good at arithmetic, feeling very excited when a problem worked out well. She'd also been blessed with a need for order and responsibility and had worked hard to pass her exams, not caring that the other girls called her a swot.

She'd started at the bank right out of school, and had taken computer courses at night school, as well as attending every course and training seminar offered by the bank. While her colleagues thought only of getting through the day so they could get home to their husbands and children, usually to put in another full day's work there, Sophie revelled in every moment on the job.

Mr Burrows, the staid old manager, thoroughly approved of Sophie, praising her in front of her workmates, which was a mixed blessing.

'Never mind them, love,' Mum soothed, when Sophie went to her with yet another tale of sneering put downs from Lacey Drew, who had started work at the branch shortly after

Sophie's arrival. 'They're just jealous. Take no notice. You'll see your day with them, my girl.'

Sophie had continued to work hard. She'd passed exams and was made Assistant Manager. She was determined that some day she'd be Branch Manager and after that, the sky was the limit.

And now old Burrows was about to retire. 'Fifty years I've been with the bank, man and boy,' he kept saying. 'Hard to believe the years have flown by so fast!' He had great plans to take up an allotment, where he hoped to count potatoes instead of money. Eager to step into his highly-polished shoes, Sophie had gone to him with her own plans.

'I don't know, I'm sure, Miss Wheeler.' Doubt was written all over his face. 'In my day, the bank would never have appointed a female manager.'

Silly old fool! She thought. This was still his day, although not for much longer. She waited patiently, until he agreed to forward her application to head office. She was delighted when she received verification that her application had been received, and that it was under consideration.

Rumour had it that the appointment would be announced today. In preparation for the great event, Sophie had dressed carefully in her new navy blue power suit and high heels. No more jumpers and skirts from now on. She had to dress the part.

A minor car crash on Broad Street meant that her bus had to be rerouted. As a result she was late arriving at work. The bank wasn't open yet, of course; the staff had to be there ahead of time to set things up before the morning rush began.

Several of her colleagues were already at their posts when she rushed in. They gave her a quick glance and looked away.

'What's the matter with everyone?' Sophie quipped. 'Cat got your tongues?'

'Mr Burrows wants to see you,' Lacey

Drew said spitefully. 'He came looking for you just now. He seemed surprised that you weren't already in. After all, this is a big day for him, isn't it? He told us to tell you that when you do show up, you're to report straight to his office. Got it?'

'Thank you, Lacey.' Sophie spoke with dignity. Somebody gave a giggle, quickly stifled.

'Ah, here you are at last, Miss Wheeler! May I introduce Mr Richard Kennedy?'

Richard Kennedy was a pleasant looking man, probably not much older than Sophie herself. About six feet tall, with straight brown hair and brown eyes, he was wearing a dark grey suit with a crisp blue shirt and a navy and red striped tie. They shook hands cordially.

'Mr Kennedy will be taking my place here,' old Burrows remarked. 'He's our newly-appointed Branch Manager.'

Richard Kennedy's lips were moving, so he must have been saying something, but Sophie couldn't make out what it was because of the buzzing in her ears. She had to pull herself together. It wouldn't do to faint on the spot.

Ah, now she knew what had happened! She was being transferred to another branch, to take up managerial duties there. That was why she'd been summoned to the inner sanctum.

'Our valued Assistant Manager,' old Burrows was saying. 'I'm sure she will give you every assistance as you settle into your new post, won't you, Miss Wheeler?'

'Yes, Mr Burrows. Of course.'

Somehow she managed to get out of the room without disgracing herself. She fled to the ladies' loo, thankful that the men couldn't follow her there. She leaned over the washbasin, the cold porcelain coming as a relief to her hot forehead.

'Are you all right, Sophie?' It was her friend, Barbara.

'I'll be all right,' Sophie muttered. 'Just leave me be for a few minutes, will you?'

'I'm not going till I know you're all right.'

'I suppose everyone knows,' Sophie said, her tone bitter.

'Well, yes, I'm afraid so. Mr Burrows made the announcement just before you got in. He introduced this Mr Kennedy to us then. I'm really sorry you didn't get the job, Sophie. I know how hard you've worked for this. Never mind, there'll be other chances, you'll see.'

'They could have told me!' Sophie muttered. 'How could old Burrows be so mean? He knew I'd applied for the job, and he must have been told about this Kennedy chap. Why didn't he put a word in my ear? Of course it would have been a disappointment, but it wouldn't have come as a nasty shock like this!'

She blinked back the tears. 'I don't know how I'm going to carry on for the rest of the day as if nothing has happened. I bet they'll all be looking at me and gloating, especially that Lacey Drew!'

'Why don't you get off home? I can say you're not feeling well.'

'Thanks, Barb, you're a pal. But no. I've got to face the rabble some time and it won't be any easier tomorrow. Go back in. I'll just wash my face and be with you in a minute.'

Head held high, she marched into her tiny cubicle and booted up her computer. Checking through her in tray while she waited for her home page to appear she came across an unopened letter, with the bank's logo in the top left hand corner. Ripping it open, breaking a fingernail in the process, she found the official response to her application.

Basically it was a 'thanks but no thanks' missive, wishing her every success in the future. She crumpled it up and hurled it towards the waste bin. Dated three days earlier, it must have come when she was out of the room at some point, and whoever had distributed the mail must have left it in her tray without telling her.

Sophie never knew how she got through that day, but at last it was over. She went home and made herself a strong cup of tea. She didn't feel like cooking; maybe she'd have a bit of toast later. All she wanted was a long soak in a bath full of bubbles, and then she'd have an early night. Tomorrow would be time enough to decide what to do.

The doorbell rang. Blast! Pretend not to be home, and whoever it was would go away. It rang again. With a groan she went to the speaker.

'Who is it?'

'It's me, James. Are you going to let me in, or what?'

'I suppose so. Come on up.'

'Charming!'

He appeared at the door, holding a bottle, wrapped in tissue paper.

'Here, you can open this. I've come to help you celebrate.'

'Drown my sorrows, is more like it.'

'What? Surely you're not telling me you didn't get the job?'

'They've appointed a man called

Richard Kennedy instead.'

'I don't believe it!' James flung himself down on the settee, still clinging to his bottle of wine. He made no attempt to remove the tissue paper, obviously not finding it worthwhile since there was nothing to celebrate now.

'It's true, James. It's the old story, I expect. This may be the New Millennium, but women still have trouble breaking through the glass ceiling.'

'Nonsense! You must have done something wrong, Soph. Not presented yourself in the best light. I told you to let me doctor your resumé. But would you listen? No. And this is the result.'

'Shut up, James! I don't need to hear this!' She walked into her bedroom, closing the door behind her.

5

'Can you believe that James actually said that to me?' Sophie demanded, as she sprawled on Kate's couch with a bottle of water clasped in her hand.

I certainly can, Kate thought, but she kept that to herself. 'I expect he felt upset on your behalf,' she murmured. 'He knew how much this promotion meant to you.'

'Oh, he was upset all right, when I threw him out of the flat! Oh, not literally, of course,' she went on, catching sight of Kate's expression, 'but I felt like doing him an injury, I can tell you. The nerve of him, telling me I don't know how to write a resumé, and that he could do better.'

'Well, he is in the PR business.'

'That's not the point. What I needed was a bit of comfort, not a lecture about my shortcomings. A hug and a kiss would have gone a long way to making me feel better. Then, get this, when I came out of the bedroom again he gave me a half hearted apology, saying he was disappointed because this might put paid to our wedding plans. Lots of people get married on less money than I'm making right now, but of course that wasn't what he meant. He still thinks he'll move into my flat after the wedding and I'll support him while he writes his book.'

'And will you?'

'I haven't decided. He'll be getting a golden handshake, so I don't see why we can't pool our resources then. Where is it written that I'd have to support my husband while he keeps his cash in the bank? It'd be different if he had health problems, or if he'd tried to get another job, but there was nothing doing.'

Was James just selfish and thick headed, or was he indeed trying to use Sophie? Kate thought that her friend would be well advised to think this through very carefully before she committed herself to marriage with him.

'What about you, Kate? Are you sticking with Mark, or are you moving on?' Sophie realised suddenly that all their talk had been about her. It was time to give her friend a hearing.

Kate sighed. 'Things are a bit up in the air at the moment. When Mark came home the other night he said he was sorry for upsetting me. He hadn't planned on saying anything in quite that way. It was just that when I brought the subject up it caught him on the hop. Then he felt he was just being cruel to be kind.'

'Ouch!'

'Ouch indeed! As you know, I felt that he was just making do with me until something better came along, but he insists it's not like that. He does love me — in his own way, I suppose — but he can't promise that he'll never fall for somebody else. He's trying to be honest, he says. Meanwhile, he doesn't want to lose me, so he's asked me not to leave.'

Sophie snorted. 'What is it with men and commitment?'

'I don't know what to do. I want to have children before it's too late. Do I stay with Mark in the hope that he'll eventually come to his senses, or do I leave now and hope to find someone new?'

'How about giving him an ultimatum, then? If you don't have a ring on your finger within six months from now, you part company.'

'That's emotional blackmail.'

'All's fair in love and war.'

Kate stood up and wandered around the room. The truth was, she wasn't prepared to make a sudden decision about whether or not to stay with Mark. She felt instinctively that it was best to let things slide for the moment. She'd said her piece; perhaps he just needed time for things to come together in his mind.

'What about your job,' she asked,

wanting to change the course of their discussion. 'Will you stay on there after what's happened? It can't be easy for you, when everyone there knows you'd applied for the top job.'

'Oh, I'll have to stay on for the moment, simply because I've no other place to go. I have to earn a living, so I can't just walk out. I may apply for a transfer later; I'll have to see.

'Meanwhile, I'm certainly not going to put myself out helping that Kennedy chap, as old Burrows suggested! I can see it now; he'll make a great success of the job based on my experience, only he'll take all the credit. Blow that for a lark!'

'You said something before about the so-called glass ceiling that prevents women in business from rising as high as men. Aren't there equal opportunity laws now? Can't you complain somewhere about this Kennedy having been parachuted in over your head?'

'He seems well qualified,' Sophie said glumly. 'For all I know, perhaps he does deserve the job. It was never promised to me, after all. What does upset me is that old Burrows never said a thing. Instead, he let me walk right into this situation. What a coward!'

'There are other jobs,' Kate murmured, but that was not what her friend needed to hear. Sophie jumped up suddenly.

'Men and work! That's enough talk about our miseries for one day! What say we indulge in a little shopping therapy, and spend, spend, spend!'

'You should be saving your pennies to get married,' Kate reproved her.

'Phooey on that. I need new shoes anyway. The heel came off one of my strappy sandals yesterday, and the cobbler says he can't do anything with it, short of taking the whole thing apart and rebuilding it.'

'Then you can shop and I'll just come and watch.'

'Surely there must be something you need?'

'Come to think of it, my milk

saucepan is a bit battered,' Kate mused. 'I suppose I could do with a new one.'

For some reason this struck them as highly amusing, and it was some time before either of them could speak again.

'The last of the big spenders!' Sophie spluttered, wiping away a tear. 'Oh, I feel a lot better for that! I say, Kate, do you remember cherry stones?'

'I remember how we loved cherries when we were little,' Kate admitted, 'especially the ones that came in pairs. We used to hang them over our ears and pretend they were earrings.'

'But the stones. You were supposed to count them to see what was in your future. Surely you remember those rhymes? 'This year, next year, some time, never?' We used to come up with some crazy ideas when we counted them out. When will I be a famous rock star? When will I have to go to the dentist and have all my teeth out?'

'My mum had a different rhyme, that was supposed to tell who you were going to marry. Don't you remember that one?

'Tinker, tailor, soldier, sailor,

Rich man, poor man, beggar man, thief.'

'Let's go out and buy cherries!' Sophie laughed. 'You could find out when Mark is going to come to his senses, and I can learn what's in the stars for me, if I decided not to hitch up with James!' Greatly cheered, they made a date to go shopping.

Reluctant to go home to an empty flat — at least, she hoped that James wasn't still hanging around there — Sophie went to call on her parents. Her father wasn't home, but her mother was there, all tea and sympathy.

'I'm sorry you didn't get the promotion you were hoping for, love, it's not the end of the world, is it? Other chances will come along. What do you mean to do now? Will you stay at the branch?'

'Oh, yes. I'm not letting that Richard Kennedy drive me away. As you say, it's just a temporary setback. I haven't failed, despite what James might say.'

Joan Wheeler picked up on this at once. 'Failed! Surely he didn't say that!'

'As good as. It appears that I don't know how to write a decent resumé. He could have made a better job of it.'

'Cheek!'

'That's what I told him. Who does he think he is, Mum? Did I tell him he was a failure when he was made redundant? No, of course I didn't. Some people have been kept on by his firm, but he wasn't one of them. If I'd chosen to get nasty I could have pointed that out.'

'Perhaps I shouldn't say this, love, but I can't help thinking that perhaps, just perhaps, James isn't the man for you. He seems so wrapped up in himself when he should be supporting you.'

'Tell me about it!'

'Yes, well, if he really cared about you he'd be out looking for another job, instead of pretending to write a book. It's my believe that's just an excuse.

He's probably lost confidence after being made redundant, and he may be afraid to go job hunting in case he's turned down again. A real man wouldn't keep marking time, he'd go out and take anything that was on offer, even some menial occupation paying minimum wage, just until something came along in his field.'

'On the other hand, if he really has a book in him, losing his job may be the perfect opportunity to get down to it,' Sophie mused, but she didn't really believe it.

6

The meeting at the library was well attended. Kate had to send Mark down to the basement to bring up extra chairs to accommodate the crowd. He had expressed an interest in attending because, as he said, he worked with older patients and knew something about their hopes and fears, and he understood what a blow it would be to the residents if Rosebank had to close.

The audience was a mixed bag of people. Kate recognised the two elderly friends who had first brought the matter of the proposed closure to her attention. They were seated in the front row, looking militant.

A reporter from The Gazette was present, looking bored. There was a frail looking woman in a wheelchair and several elderly persons with zimmer frames parked beside them. Possibly these were Rosebank people; the home's minibus was parked outside the front entrance.

The meeting was called to order by a tall man with a brush of white hair. He identified himself as Colonel Browning, chairman of the Save Rosebank Committee.

'Are you a resident of the home, sir?' This was The Gazette reporter, eager to get off on the right foot.

'No, I am not!' the colonel barked. 'I'm simply doing my public duty as a member of the community. It's utterly disgraceful that a place like Rosebank should be threatened with closure, when what we need are even more such facilities.'

'Hear, hear!'

He acknowledged his supporters with a curt nod and then began to rhyme off statistics about how the baby boomers were ageing and before long there would be more senior citizens in Britain than there were younger people to look after them, either physically or financially.

Kate's attention began to wander. She glanced over at Mark, who was listening with rapt attention. When there was a lull in the proceedings he jumped to his feet and began an impassioned speech, which had the onlookers leaning forward in their seats.

'We've got to stem the tide before it's too late!' he declared. 'Don't you realise how many such facilities are closing down these days?'

'Most of our senior citizens have worked hard all their lives.'

When Mark had stopped, Kate noticed that a ruddy-faced man in the back row was waving his hand in some agitation.

'The chair recognises Mr Carseley.'

All eyes swivelled in his direction as the man lumbered to his feet, clearing his throat.

'It's the owner of Rosebank!' Kate's assistant hissed. 'I didn't know he was coming. Talk about walking into the lion's den!'

'I know what you're all thinking,'

Carseley began. 'You've got me down as the villain of the piece. Well, let me tell you, it hasn't been easy, coming to this decision. My wife and I,' here he looked down at the stout woman sitting at his side, 'Sheila and I have spent many a sleepless night tossing this back and forth. The fact of the matter is, we're losing money hand over fist on this venture and it can't go on, or one of these days we're going to find ourselves in the poor house.'

'You people charge enough!' someone called out. 'I should know; you've got my old mother in there, and it takes more than her pension to keep her there, that's for sure.'

'Even so, the fees don't come close to covering the costs, madam. Everything keeps going up and up. The cost of electricity, staff wages, even the price of food.'

'Somebody is making a fat profit,' she insisted. 'I could keep her at home for less than half of what we shell out to you.'

'Then I suggest you do, madam. In fact, you'd better be prepared to do just that, because all the residents will be receiving notices shortly. We'll be closing down at the end of next month.'

'Isn't there something you can do to make ends meet?' Kate asked, caught up in the drama.

'Just what would you suggest? Feed people bread and scraps instead of well-balanced meals? Sack the staff and bring in untrained personnel?'

'Perhaps there could be a drive to raise funds?' This suggestion was met with a round of applause, but Carseley only shrugged. He had made up his mind and clearly he wasn't interested in any stop-gap measures.

When he walked out of the room, with his wife in tow, there was silence for a few moments until Mark spoke up again.

'We're not giving up without a fight, are we?'

'Not much we can do, is there?' the wheelchair woman sniffed. 'Their sort always wins. And if they can't afford to carry on, well, that's it, isn't it?'

'Not if we mount a proper campaign. We can start by picketing the place. That will get us in the news. I'm sure The Gazette will cover the event, and with any luck we can get the local television people involved, too.'

'Could get national coverage,' the reporter agreed. 'This sort of thing isn't just a local issue, see. It's probably happening all over the country, or will do before long.'

He could see himself on to a good thing, selling news items to the big dailies.

Before the evening was over, Mark had been appointed to the Save Rosebank Committee. He was full of plans and enthusiasm as they headed home.

'I'm glad you feel so strongly about this issue,' Kate told him, 'but do you really think we can do any good?'

'Never say die!' he replied. 'As a nurse, I know quite a bit about the issues involved here, and I'm committed to doing all I can. You know, Kate,' he went on, 'I'd really like to run my own retirement home one day. It's the coming thing, with our population ageing by leaps and bounds, and good carers will never be out of a job. On top of that, I'd be doing a real service to humanity.'

His eyes were glowing with fervour and a great wave of love for him surged through her. Mark was everything she wanted in a husband; hard working, concerned about his fellow man, ready to stand up for what he believed in. Not like James Simpson, who was all out for himself.

James! An idea came to her.

'I say, why don't you bring James Simpson on board?'

'Who?'

'James Simpson, the chap Sophie's engaged to. He's in Public Relations. He might be able to help your campaign. He's been trained in how to present things in the best possible light.

He should know the right approach to take in a situation like this.'

'Is that his name? But would he have the time? I thought you said he was writing a book?'

'Supposed to be, but he can't work on it twenty-four hours a day, seven days a week, can he?'

'It can't hurt to try. Go ahead then, sound him out if you want.'

It was Sophie whom Kate approached first. Sophie was doubtful in the beginning.

'You know what he's like, Kate. Unless there's something in it for him, he won't want to know.'

'Ah, but here's what you tell him. If he gets involved with this, think how wonderful it will look on his resumé when he wants to get back to his old line of work. Public-spirited chap, working for the good of others, even when he's been made redundant. He might even get himself seen on telly, and that can't do him any harm.

'I'll put it to him, and see what he

says, but just what are you up to, Kate Kent?'

Kate shrugged. 'I want the Save Rosebank Campaign to succeed. Not just for the residents, although that's the most important thing, of course. Mark is all fired up about this and I want to show him I'm right there to support him. I'm sure James will be a real asset to the team.'

'Which will make Mark realise how valuable you are as a partner,' Sophie agreed. 'Nothing wrong with that, I suppose. And you're right; this could be just what James needs. I'll speak to him tonight and see what he says. I may, of course, get my head bitten off, but I can live with that.'

7

Chip McNaughton waited with growing impatience while the news editor handed out assignments for the week. He was eager to get his teeth into something interesting but so far Branksome seemed like a one horse town. He was beginning to regret having come here, although in his more rational moments he realised that he was lucky to have a job at all.

New journalism grads were two a penny, and most newspapers had eager beginners practically lining up at the doors, willing to work for free to gain experience. It was the old story. Employers wouldn't take you on unless you had experience, but how could you get it if they wouldn't hire you?

'McNaughton!'

'Yes, Chief?'

'I want you to stay on this Rosebank

story. Get out there and interview some of the old folk. Write up a few sob stories, you know the sort of thing.'

Chip nodded. It wouldn't make for deathless prose, but it was all grist to his mill. If the story took off and reached the nationals, he might be able to sell some human-interest bits. He might even get a byline.

'And McNaughton, keep your ears open for anything that doesn't sound quite right at Rosebank.'

'Like what?'

'Like why the place is slated to close, rather than being sold. Get on to the Health Department and see if they've had any problems on that side of things. Go to the town hall and find out if there are any structural problems at the home. Nineteenth century buildings take a lot of keeping up. Who knows, it could be that the place is on the verge of being condemned.'

'Right, Chief.'

'And in your spare time you can get on to this Save Rosebank Committee.

Do a few bios of the people serving on it. Find out what their interest is. That Roberts chap, for instance. He's a nurse; there may be an angle there. I'm not saying we'll print the lot, mind, but we should have something in reserve in case it's a slow week.'

Chip decided to pursue the Health and Safety issues first. Hard news always took precedence over features. The human-interest stuff could wait.

Of course, people in authority often played their cards close to their chests. He recalled what his college lecturer was fond of saying. 'Lateral thinking, my boy. Lateral thinking!'

Luckily Chip had a foot in the door in the Planning Department at the town hall. The secretary there was a girl he'd taken out once or twice. He'd take her out to lunch; it would be money well spent if he could worm something out of her. Or, if the story was good enough, he might even be able to charge it up to expenses. Whistling, he went out to his battered Volkswagen.

Mary Jane accompanied him to the Copper Kettle willingly enough, but when he tried to raise the subject of Rosebank she clammed up.

'I'm not supposed to discuss confidential matters outside the office,' she said primly.

'Come on, Mary Jane, this is me you're talking to!'

'Exactly! Anything I tell you will appear in The Gazette and I'll get the sack!'

'I won't quote you.'

'Oh, right! My boss isn't stupid. He'll know where the leak is.'

More than that she refused to say. 'Lateral thinking!' Chip thought.

'Oh, well, never mind all that. I don't suppose it's very interesting, anyway. How about coming out for a drink after work on Thursday?'

'Why Thursday?'

'No reason, except that Friday's my day off. It won't matter if I'm out late because I don't have to get up at the crack of dawn the next day.'

'Oh. OK, then, I don't mind if I do.'

Weekends and evenings were the busiest times at a weekly newspaper because that was when the rest of the world indulged in meetings and recreational activities which were covered by the reporting staff. Hence days off were given during the week.

Mary Jane was already aware of that. What she couldn't know was that Chip's time off had nothing to do with what he was planning, which was to get her tipsy and pick her brain while she was off guard.

* * *

While waiting for the library to open its doors, Kate Kent was typing up an agenda for the forthcoming committee meeting. Mark had invited the group to get together in their flat, with the idea that they were less likely to be interrupted there than if they met in the library.

Not for the first time she blessed the

day that computers were invented. She could print out any number of copies in a matter of minutes, so different from the days of typewriters and carbon paper, and each one looked crisp and professional.

She herself wasn't on the committee, but she'd been an interested observer, especially if Griff Hargreaves was going to be there!

He was a successful writer of crime novels, which simply flew off the shelves at the library. The most unlikely people were always coming in and asking if 'the new Griff Hargreaves' was in yet.

He lived about twenty miles away, but as soon as he'd heard about Rosebank's problems he'd rung up and offered his services. Mark had been delighted when Kate had passed this on.

'He's so well known for his involvement in green issues and working with the underdog, Kate! This will really add something to the cause when the papers get wind of this. I bet he'll have some good ideas, too, after everything he's done in the past.'

'I'm delighted, too,' Kate confided to Sophie. 'If I get to know him well enough, maybe I can persuade him to give a talk at the library some evening. He doesn't do that as a rule. I gather he's so busy with his good causes, and churning out a new book each year, that he just doesn't have time. It would be a feather in my cap if I could get him to come.'

Sophie mentioned this latest development casually to James. He brightened at once.

'Sounds as if this committee is really going places! I've given some thought to what you said before, and I've decided to join them. I must do my bit for the community.'

'James!' Sophie was delighted. 'I'll let Kate know, shall I? She's already invited me to go to her flat, as an onlooker, and I'm quite looking forward to it.' A thought struck her. 'What made you change your mind? I thought you'd be too busy getting on with your book.'

'Well, if an important author like Griff Hargreaves can do it, I should get on side as well. We writers must stick together and all that!'

We writers! As far as Sophie knew, James hadn't yet put pen to paper, although in his case perhaps the expression should be fingers to key-board. She'd have given a lot to get a peep at his laptop to see exactly what he was doing. Why, she didn't even know what sort of novel he was planning to write.

'Are you interested in crime fiction, then?' she asked innocently. 'Have you started work on something like that?'

'I haven't decided yet. I'm still considering my options.

'I've heard that people should write about what they know. Why don't you write a novel about the cut and thrust in a Public Relations firm? Plenty of possibilities there.'

'That setting would do for all sorts of things, from a thriller to a romance.'

'Mmm. Hargreaves may be able to give me some ideas.'

'James! You can't ask him that!'

'Why on earth not? He knows the ropes. Why should he quibble at giving me some useful tips?'

Sophie could think of several good reasons why not, but she knew better than to voice them. Now she knew why James was so eager to get involved with the committee. He wasn't the slightest bit interested in helping the residents of Rosebank who were faced with the prospect of losing their home.

He wanted to get close to the famous author, for his own ends. She would be so embarrassed if he accosted Griff during the meeting with all sorts of questions that had nothing to do with the issue at hand.

'Perhaps you should wait a bit before you speak to him,' she ventured. 'When you have something concrete to discuss with him, I mean. These meetings are likely to go on for some time, and you'll have the chance to really get to know him. He's more likely to offer help if he's come to know you as a friend.'

She chided herself for being insincere, but James seemed to take her remarks at face value.

'Good thinking,' he told her. 'Then I can get him to read my manuscript and give me his opinion. He might even send it to his agent.'

Sophie suppressed a sigh. Did James never see the world in any way that was not of benefit for him? She only hoped that Griff Hargreaves was capable of defending himself, once he came up against James in full cry.

8

Things were settling down at work. Apart from some nasty hints thrown in her direction by Lacey Drew, Sophie found that her failure to obtain the top job was a non-issue. Not that failure was the way to describe it, she reminded herself. Although she'd been unsuccessful — this time around — she'd done her best, and just because someone else was better qualified, or had done a better job of impressing the powers that be, she had nothing to be ashamed of. James had no right to add to her disappointment by making her feel she'd fallen short.

Richard Kennedy had already proved himself as a boss who was worthy of the job. Firm but fair, he had the staff eating out of his hand. All but Sophie, that was. She did her work with her usual efficiency, and she responded to any request he made without putting obstacles in his way, but she wasn't about to fall all over him like some of the others.

Thus it came as a shock to her when he invited her out for a drink after work.

'I'm sorry, I can't.' She hadn't meant to sound so abrupt, but that was how the words came out.

'How about tomorrow evening instead, then?'

'I'm afraid not.' She crossed her fingers behind her back. 'I'm engaged to be married, you know. My fiancé wouldn't like it.'

'Surely he can't object to your having one drink with a colleague, in broad daylight? There are a few things I'd like to discuss with you, about work, of course.'

She felt silly then. She'd jumped to the conclusion that he was inviting her on a sort of date, although surely professional matters could have been talked over in his office, during working hours.

'I'm sorry,' she stammered. 'I didn't think you meant . . . ' Red-faced, she tried to find some way out of this awkward situation. 'I've got an important meeting to go to tomorrow night, and James, my boyfriend, is going too. It's about saving Rosebank.'

'Where, or what, is Rosebank?'

'Oh, I forgot that you're new in town. Rosebank is a rather nice privately-owned retirement home. The owners are giving up and naturally the residents are all very upset. They'd expected to live out the rest of their lives there, and now they're about to be made homeless.'

'Most unpleasant,' he agreed. 'Perhaps I can be of some help.'

'You? What can you do?'

'I am a bank manager, remember. If financial advice is needed, I'm your man.'

'I work in banking, too,' Sophie reminded him, 'although not as high up the scale as you! I know as much about loans and mortgages as the next man.'

She caught a glimpse of her reflection in the glass partition. Her face wore the sort of expression the Queen might have if one of the corgis presented her unexpectedly with a dead rat. She managed to raise a smile.

'Thanks for the offer, Richard. I'll pass it on to the committee.'

This encounter left her feeling thoroughly unsettled, so instead of going directly home after work she went to see her parents.

'This is a nice surprise,' Joan Wheeler said. 'There's nothing wrong, is there?'

'Why should anything be wrong?' Sophie countered, in some irritation. Why was that always Mum's first question when she visited or rang up? They saw each other at least twice a week; it wasn't as if she lived a hundred miles away. She was relieved when her father entered the room. At least he wasn't always imagining upsets and disasters.

'Work going all right, is it? How are you getting on with your new boss?'

'All right, I suppose. I put my foot in it today, though. He asked me out for a drink, and like a fool I thought it was meant to be a date.'

'And it wasn't?'

'No, Mum. It was to talk about work stuff. At least, that was what he said when I mentioned James.'

'Speaking of James, how is he?' Bert Wheeler interrupted. 'Any job prospects on the horizon?'

'I don't think he's really looking, Dad. He hasn't much longer to go at Fraser & Dickens, so it must be on his mind, but if he does have plans, he won't discuss them with me. I tried bringing the subject up last night, and he just about bit my head off.'

'That's because he's worried about his future, poor boy,' Joan remarked.

'Worried about whether I mean to support him while he writes his wretched novel, Mum. I haven't actually said anything to him yet, but I'm simply not going to do it, especially now that I didn't get my promotion, and the pay rise that went with it.'

Bert thumped the kitchen table with his fist, making them jump. 'Good on yer, girl! No real man would want his wife to support him while he fiddled around stringing words together!'

'You're behind the times, Dad. That isn't how it works, nowadays. Lots of men stay home to look after the kids while their wives carry on with a career.'

'That's got nothing to do with your situation, and you know it. And I may be a bit of a dinosaur, but I can still see the way this is likely to pan out! He'll live off you until your savings run out, and then he'll move on to greener pastures. My advice to you, my girl, is to get a ring on your finger before you allow James Simpson to back you into a corner like that!'

Joan stood up. 'Now, Bert! Let's not start an argument. I'll make us a nice cup of tea, shall I, and we'll find something better to talk about. We don't see as much of Sophie as we'd like, so let's not spoil the time we do spend together.'

He mumbled something that she couldn't catch. Having lived with him for as long as she had, she was sure it wasn't something complimentary. When the tea was made, and they were sitting at the table with their steaming cups in front of them, she attempted to pour oil on troubled waters.

'I imagine that James will receive quite a good redundancy package from his firm? That should be enough to keep him for a year or so, if he's careful, and by that time he'll have his book finished and he'll be rolling in money. Then you two can get married, and settle down.'

Her husband made a rude noise.

'Oh, Mum!' Sophie sighed. 'If only it was that simple. To start with, I don't even know if James has written so much as a word yet, and even if he does have a good idea and can summon up the expertise to follow through to the end, there are no guarantees.'

'Surely all he has to do is send the manuscript to a publisher, who'll take it from there? Or perhaps he can get one of those, what do they call them, agents to deal with the business side of things?'

'There's a bit more to it than that, according to Kate. There's a book in the library called *How To Write And Sell Your Novel*, and she's read it. Apparently a first novel has to be pretty good to get taken on by a publisher, and even then the financial rewards may be small, and a long time coming. I hope that James is being realistic about it, but somehow I doubt it.'

'But look at J. K. Rowling,' Joan protested. 'It's worked out marvellously for her!'

'I don't care if the chap is Arthur Conan Doyle come back to life!' Bert snapped. 'He's not good enough for our Sophie, and that's a fact.'

'Oh, Bert! You think that nobody's good enough for your little girl, short of an earl or a duke! You've always been the same. Remember when she started going out with that boy from Kingsley Street? You said he was a long-haired idiot who'd never amount to a hill of beans.'

'Mum! Dad! Just stop it, will you? I hate it when you wrangle like this. I'm a big girl now. I can run my own life, thanks very much!'

Her father was determined to have the last word. 'As I've said before, the best thing you can do, my girl, is kick that Simpson chap into touch!'

Sophie leapt to her feet. 'This has been very nice, but I've got to get to the launderette before it closes. I haven't a clean blouse to wear to work tomorrow. Thanks for the tea, Mum.' They heard the door slam behind her.

'What's the girl talking about? As far as I know the launderette stays open until ten o'clock six nights a week.'

'Bert Wheeler! Can't you see she just didn't want to listen to you ranting on?'

'I don't care. The chap's not good enough and you know it.'

'I'm beginning to think that myself,

and I hope she'll see the light before it's too late. But if you carry on like this you'll drive her right into his arms, and then the fat will be in the fire. She's likely to turn up here some day on his arm, telling us that they've eloped or something.'

'Nonsense!'

'It's not nonsense. She's feeling vulnerable right now since not getting that promotion she wanted so badly, and she might just fall in with James Simpson's plans because it looks like the easiest option. Go carefully, Bert, or we may lose her.'

* * *

'Have you seen this?' Kate passed the newspaper to Mark as they sat at the table, finishing their breakfast. The Gazette had done Rosebank proud, with a full-page spread featuring interviews with the residents, complete with photos. She proceeded to tell him what the retirees had said.

'That one's a Mary James. She was so lonely after her husband died, she didn't know where to turn. Then she managed to scrape up the money to go to Rosebank, and everything changed. She made new friends there and thought she'd have them for the rest of her days. She's absolutely dreading the idea of having to start all over again.

'And look, here's a pitiful story of some lady with nowhere else to go. Her daughter can't have her, because she's got a husband and six kids, all squashed into a nineteen thirties semi, and they can't fit a budgie in, never mind poor old Grandma. All the state facilities have long waiting lists, so where does that leave her? ''I don't want to become a bag lady, at my age,' seventy-six year old Aggie Rothwell sobs'.'

Kate shuddered. She wondered where she'd be forty years from now. She paid into a pension scheme, of course, but how far would the money stretch when the time came for her to stop work? People were already being warned to save for retirement if they hoped to maintain any sort of decent lifestyle.

'Do you really think there's any hope of persuading the Carseleys to stay on?'

'That's why we formed this committee, to consider our options. A fund raising campaign is one possibility. Their main complaint is that they can't carry on as they are without cutting back drastically on services. I suspect they're fed up with operating at a loss or close to it and I can't say I blame them. They're ordinary people, not saints after all.'

'But if funds do come from the community, what guarantee would you have that the cash doesn't go straight into the Carseleys' pockets instead of being put to good use for the residents?'

'I'm hoping that Kennedy will have some ideas about that. Proper accounting, let's say, or some sort of trust fund.'

'Do you mean Richard Kennedy? Sophie's new boss?'

'That's the chap. He took me aside

when I went into the bank to deposit my pay cheque. Said he'd heard about it from Sophie and wanted to help.'

'I wonder how she'll feel about that? There's no love lost between them from what I can gather.'

The library was always in need of money and she had seen many such efforts come and go. It would take more than a few bake sales and raffles to save Rosebank from closure.

'I've just had a worrying thought,' Mark mused. 'Why aren't the Carseleys selling Rosebank?'

'I'm not sure what you mean.'

'I don't know why this hasn't occurred to anyone before this. Surely they want some return on their investment, so why close it down?'

'I imagine they'll put the building up for sale, won't they?'

'No doubt they will, but I wonder why they haven't tried to sell the business as a going concern. They might do even better then.'

Kate shrugged. 'Any private buyer

would have to be pretty well heeled to afford it. Rosebank is a huge old house; set in goodness knows how many acres of land. I'd say the Carseleys are sitting on a gold mine.'

'Exactly. And if I were in their shoes I'd be trying to get as much out of it as possible, after years of running the place on a shoestring. Surely one of those commercial chains of nursing homes might be interested? That is, unless . . . '

'Unless what?'

'Can't stop to discuss it now, Kate. If I don't get off right this minute I'll be late for work, and that would never do!' He grabbed his backpack and hurried out. She stared after him, bemused. She couldn't fathom what he was thinking, but she was glad to see him so animated.

It was quite like the old days, before they'd moved in together. He'd always been so full of enthusiasm about everything he did, but lately he'd turned into a plodder, moving from home to work and back again, rarely getting excited about anything. She'd worried about this, believing that the spark had gone out of their relationship. Was it anything to do with her?

Was he regretting asking her to live with him? She'd done everything she could think of to keep them together but lately she'd wondered if it was enough.

Now this new occupation had brought back the sparkle to his eyes. Perhaps his recent moodiness had nothing to do with her, after all. He loved his job, but nursing could be a stressful business at times, especially when, despite their best efforts, a patient died. Everyone, not only nurses, needed outside interests if they were to stay on an even keel, and if this Save Rosebank Campaign was what Mark needed to revive his flagging spirits, it couldn't have come at a better time.

Chip McNaughton was doing his best to dig up the dirt on Rosebank, but so far, nothing doing. Repeated visits to the Health Department had yielded nothing of interest; the latest inspection of the facility had resulted in a glowing report, with not so much as a faulty drain to complain about.

He was afraid that his story would fizzle out to nothing more than the few human-interest pieces he'd done; a few grannies shoved out in the cold with nowhere to go. Regrettable, he supposed, but unfortunately nothing new.

'Come up with something in the next forty-eight hours or I'm pulling you off this non-story,' his editor warned, making Chip redouble his efforts. He was fed up with covering flower shows and town council meetings. Was it for this he had slogged his way through college?

He had one last chance, and that was Mary Jane Evans. He had no compunction about taking her out in order to pick her brains. If she read more into it than that, it was her problem. She was a giggler, and he detested women who laughed for no good reason. She certainly wasn't his type. He much preferred the peroxide blonde at the Ploughman's Arms, but she already had a boyfriend, a bricklayer the size of the houses he worked on.

★   ★   ★

'I'll have another Port and lemon, please,' Mary Jane simpered.

Chip winced. This wasn't going well. This was the third drink he'd had to buy her, and they hadn't got round to the subject of Rosebank at all. So far she had plied him with questions about his work. Showing an interest, of course. She'd probably read in some magazine that this was the way to hook a man.

Returning with their drinks, he plastered a false smile on his face. 'Enough about me! Tell me about your work. It's an important job, I'm sure.'

She simpered again. 'Not really. My mum was a shorthand typist in the old days and nothing much has changed, except that now I work with a word processor. All I do is take notes at meetings and type things up.'

'But you do know what's going on, then.'

'Of course I do, but it's all confidential, see? No good you asking me how much the department spends on tea bags in any given week!'

'I wouldn't dream of asking! I do wonder how many tea bags they use at Rosebank, though. I'm working on a story about that place. It appears that the owners are having difficulty making ends meet.' He was being facetious, of course, so he was greatly surprised by what came next.

Mary Jane opened her myopic eyes very wide. 'Oh, but it won't matter, will it? Rosebank won't be there very much longer.'

'What do you mean?'

'Well, it's going to be pulled down, isn't it? There's dozens of new houses going up on that land, p'raps as many as a hundred. Whoever lives there will have to buy their own tea bags in future.

'Pardon!' She gave a little hiccup. 'Oh, dear, that's supposed to be a secret. You won't tell anyone what I said, will you?'

'I won't breathe a word,' he lied.

9

Chip McNaughton stole a wary look at the clock, which was steadily ticking the hours away above the bar. He hadn't finished with Mary Jane yet, but it wouldn't do to make her late getting back to work. Questions might be asked and it would never do to create a trail, which might lead her bosses back to him.

'You do promise, don't you?' Mary Jane was staring at him with a look of pleading in her big brown eyes.

'I never reveal my sources,' Chip assured her. He certainly wasn't about to keep quiet about the proposed housing development, but neither did he want to land the poor girl in trouble. She would certainly lose her job if it were known that she had blurted out confidential information, and even though he was using her to some extent, deep down he wasn't an uncaring individual. Or so he liked to believe.

'What's the name of this development company, Mary Jane?'

'Oh, I don't think I'd better say, Chip. I've told you too much already.'

'Then it won't hurt to give me just this one thing more, will it? Come on, Mary Jane, you can tell Uncle Chip! I don't see that it's such a big secret, anyhow, if Rosebank's about to close.'

Back at The Gazette office, Chip felt quite pleased with himself. Booting up his computer he prepared an e-mail to send to Mike Collins, his old room mate from college days. Mike had a knack of finding out information, which certain people hoped to keep hidden from prying eyes. As Chip knew from past experience, it was better not to enquire too deeply into his methods, but Mike owed him a favour or two, and now was the time to call one of these in.

In a surprisingly short time, he

received an e-mail, which had a very interesting attachment. He printed it out and went in search of his editor.

'So according to you, Rosebank isn't slated to close because it's too expensive to run,' the editor frowned, 'but because some big development group wants the land it's sitting on.'

'Yes, chief. They plan to build hundreds of houses there.'

'They might let the house remain there, don't you think? I've seen that happen before. Someone with an old family home, often falling to bits, sells off the land to make some ready cash, with the provision that the old mansion stays where it is.'

Chip shook his head. 'I've got hold of this brochure they're about to send out to their investors. It shows exactly what they mean to build after the home is reduced to rubble.'

'I won't ask you where you got hold of that, my boy. It smacks of something illegal to me. You haven't got into computer hacking, I hope.'

This was coming too close for comfort, and Chip chose to ignore it. 'Just take a look at this,' he went on. 'It's not only houses they're going to build. There'll be a pretty comprehensive shopping mall nearby, as well as a community centre complete with a spa and gym. People who move in there won't have to come into town to do their shopping, or anything else.'

'Whew! By the sound of this we're not talking about cheap little houses where you can hear everything the neighbours are saying next door!'

'That's the whole point. The next page of this brochure has an architect's mock up showing one of the proposed homes with a two-car garage and a sizable bit of acreage all round. There's a fat profit to be made when this development goes through.'

'Let's not rush to any conclusions here, Chip. What I don't understand is why all the secrecy? What's the name of that couple who operate Rosebank? Carseleys? Why bleat about not being able to make ends meet? Why not be up front about it and say they've got the chance to sell out at a nice profit, so they're off to a comfortable retirement in Spain?'

'I suppose they think they'll have a riot on their hands if they let slip what's really going on. Better to get the old folks moved out before the penny drops.'

'Maybe; maybe not. I tell you one thing, though; this is going to put the cat among the pigeons at the town hall. Before any sale can go through, they'll have to get planning permission. Rosebank may have to be rezoned, too. A major housing development is a far cry from a genteel retirement home for little old ladies.'

The editor studied his fingernails for a long moment before continuing his train of thought. 'Yes, people will be up in arms, no doubt about it. It'll start more trouble than this town has seen since the time of the Civil War! Some people will be all for it. Think of the work it will make for local contractors and tradesmen. Prosperity comes to town, that sort of thing.'

'And the traditionalists will be dead against it.' Chip nodded. 'The development won't do a thing for local shopkeepers when this fancy mall gets up and running. In fact, it may take away some of the custom they have now, because everyone will be trooping out to Rosebank to see what's going on.'

'Either way, it'll do our circulation some good. We may as well start the ball rolling now. This is front-page material, my boy. You write up your story and if it's a good one I'll see that you get a prominent byline. See if you can hold off the Carseleys for a comment, but never mind if they won't talk. A 'not available for comment' will make it look as if they've something to hide.'

Chip was well pleased with himself. The continuing saga would probably run for some weeks and it was his baby.

One after the other the committee members arrived at the flat, where Kate and Mark were waiting to receive them. Colonel Browning first, early as usual, his military training making it impossible for him to turn up late for anything.

Then Sophie waltzed in, accompanied by James, whose eyes darted round the room in anticipation of finding Griff Hargreaves already on the spot. Miss Robson and Mrs Philpotts were there as representatives of the Rosebank residents.

Griff Hargreaves poked his head round the door a few minutes later. Kate noted with interest that he looked considerably older than he did in the photo, which graced the dust covers of his books. Probably he'd had it taken when he first started out and had never seen any reason to change it.

'I'm not late, am I?' he asked apologetically. 'The phone rang just as I was leaving the house, and I felt I had to answer it. Then of course it was some woman who babbled on about nothing, and I didn't want to cut her off, because you have to be nice to your fans, or bang go your future sales.'

'You should get yourself an answering machine,' Sophie told him, earning herself a glare from James.

'Can't abide the things. I used to have one, but after it blew up I never got around to replacing it.' He grinned at her appealingly, and James looked taken aback.

'Are we all here?' the colonel asked. 'No, I can see that reporter chappie isn't here. Well, that's his bad luck. We'll start without him and he'll just have to catch up later. Haven't got time to waste, sitting around doing nothing.'

But at that moment the doorbell rang, and Kate went to answer it, surprised to find Chip standing there with bundles of newspapers under his arm.

'Sorry I'm late, folks! There's something here I know you'll want to see. Tomorrow's paper, hot off the press!'

He distributed pristine copies of The Gazette, oblivious to the puzzled glances of those present.

'What is this all about, Mr McNaughton?' Mrs Philpotts was fishing for her spectacles in an oversized handbag. 'Don't tell me the Carseleys have had a change of heart? Why weren't we told this first, instead of having to read it in the newspaper?'

'Have a look at page one,' Chip said proudly. 'It explains everything pretty well, if I do say so myself.'

There was absolute silence for a few moments as those present searched for the relevant piece and digested its contents.

'Well, of all the blinking nerve!' Mark burst out.

'Just hold your horses for a moment,' the colonel interrupted. 'I want to read this through a second time, to make sure I've got it straight in my mind.'

'I've read it three times,' Mrs Philpotts insisted, 'but I still don't know what it means.'

'It means,' said James coldly, 'that we're all wasting our time. Rosebank was doomed from the outset. These people never had any intention of allowing your home to carry on. All they're interested in is feathering their own nest.' He smiled unpleasantly at the two elderly ladies as he delivered this coup de grace.

'This time next year Rosebank will be a distant memory, and lots of pretty little houses will be springing up in its place. Absolutely nothing can be done to save it.'

'Oh, lor!' whispered little Miss Robson. 'So what do we do now?'

⋆ ⋆ ⋆

The bank had closed for the day, and most of the staff had gone home. Sophie was still at her desk, tidying up a few remaining jobs. Richard Kennedy appeared in the entrance to her cubicle.

'I'm just brewing up. Fancy a cuppa?'

'Oh, yes, please. I'm dying for one.

Milk, no sugar.'

'Coming right up!' He disappeared.

This was something new; a man waiting on her for a change! Even her father tended to ask Mum if there was any chance of a brew, rather than troubling to put the kettle on himself.

Richard reappeared, carrying a mug in each hand. Sophie took a sip and gave a sigh of contentment. The man certainly knew how to make a good cup of tea.

'So how did the meeting go last night?' he asked. 'Do they want me to come on board, then?'

Oh, dear! In all the turmoil, which followed Chip's bombshell, nobody had given any thought to Richard's offer of help. After all, it looked as if the Save Rosebank Campaign was dead in the water. Obtaining financial advice was the least of their worries.

'Obviously you haven't seen The Gazette this morning,' she told him.

'The Gazette? No, I haven't picked one up yet. Why, is there something about Rosebank in it?'

'You could say that. It appears that the land is in the process of being sold to a big development company, who plan to put a whole housing complex there in its place, including a shopping mall and a community centre.'

'Whew!' Richard let out a long, low whistle. 'It'll take more than a handful of letters to the editor and a few supporters on the picket line to stop that lot!'

'Exactly. So you can imagine how finding that out threw everyone into confusion. Even old Colonel Browning was at a loss. In the end he said they'd better adjourn to think things over, and reconvene again at a later date. The only person who got any satisfaction out of that meeting was James!'

'James?'

'My fiancé. He's writing a novel; at least, he says he is. I don't know if he's begun work on it yet. He was pretty excited when he heard that Griff Hargreaves had volunteered to serve on the committee.'

'Oh, the man who writes thrillers. He's pretty good. I have a few of his paperbacks myself. I take it that your James is a fan?'

'I don't know about that. All he's interested in is picking the man's brains. He had him pinned in a corner last night, asking him all sorts of questions about how to get published and how much money he can expect to make from a first novel. I was so embarrassed I couldn't get out of there fast enough.'

'But what was wrong with that? Networking is the name of the game nowadays. If Hargreaves didn't like being put on the spot, surely he could have given James a polite brush off?'

Sophie threw up her hands. 'It's just that James is such a user. People might be more willing to help him if his every action wasn't calculated to benefit himself in some way.'

Richard looked at her for a long moment, saying nothing. Then he bit his lip before voicing what was on his mind.

'You'll forgive me for asking, I hope, but you don't have a ring on your finger, Sophie. Of course, if you just became engaged recently and the pair of you haven't had time to choose a ring yet, that's one thing, but somehow I gather that there's been, how can I put it, a rift in the lute?'

'What a funny expression! I'm sorry if I've given you the wrong impression. I shouldn't have talked about James like that. It's so disloyal.'

'Sometimes it helps to talk to a friend. You can feel free to talk to me, Sophie. Think of me as your Uncle Richard, if you like.'

She felt a warm glow at his words. He regarded her as a friend! A little of the ice around her frozen heart seemed to thaw slightly.

'I really shouldn't . . . '

'I think you should let me know what's going on. After all, if you're getting married soon and thinking of leaving the bank, that will have an impact on me.'

Suddenly she found herself blurting out the whole sorry tale. How James was being made redundant and was planning to use this down time to craft the novel he'd always wanted to write.

'Actually, that sounds good to me. If they give him a pretty decent golden handshake, what's wrong with following his dream? He could give himself a year or two to find out if he's got a book in him, and if that doesn't work out he can return to his present profession. Don't you think you're being a bit hard on the man, Sophie?'

'Not at all. And if you want to know why, it's because his dream is my nightmare!'

'I don't understand.'

'No, because you don't know the whole story. We've been seeing each other James and me for four years, Richard. Four years, when it didn't seem to be going anywhere. Now he's decided we should get married, on the 'two can live as cheaply as one' principle. He wants to move into my flat, and I'm supposed to keep him while he does his own thing. If I thought he loved me I'd be happy to work my fingers to the bone for him, but that doesn't seem to be the case. All I am to him is a meal ticket, and no woman wants to be used.'

'But do you love him?' Richard asked softly.

'I honestly don't know any more. I thought I did, but now I'm confused, torn two ways. On one hand there's James, demanding an answer as soon as possible, and on the other there's my mother, wanting her only daughter to have a fabulous wedding, one which will take time to pull off.'

'And what do you want, Sophie?'

'Well, of course I want a proper wedding. It doesn't have to be an expensive do, but I want my family and friends around me when it happens. None of that seems to matter to James.'

'I think that in your heart you already know the solution,' Richard said slowly. 'If you loved him desperately you'd do anything to be with him, go to the ends of the earth if you had to. If you can't make up your mind you should let him off the hook.'

Sophie was about to make a sharp retort when she caught sight of Richard's face. The look of utter sadness in his eyes made her gulp.

'You sound as if you know what you're talking about, Richard. Have you felt like that about someone, then?'

'Um, well, since this would appear to be true confessions time, I suppose that deserves an answer. Yes, I've been in love, the sort of happiness that only comes along once in a lifetime. I was engaged to a beautiful girl named Rachel, but six months before the wedding she died.'

Sophie flinched. 'That's dreadful! What on earth happened, a car accident?'

'Cancer. A very fast growing type that wasn't diagnosed until it was too late. Even so I still wanted to marry her, of course I did, but she refused.

She kept saying she wanted me to remember her as she was, not to have to spend every day living with her in pain and distress. She tried to make me go away, Sophie. Pleaded with me, in fact.'

'But you didn't.'

'Of course not! How could I? I couldn't force her to marry me, but I could visit her each day at the hospice. I was with her when she died, Sophie. In the end she just faded away.'

Sophie could not find the words to respond. What is there to say in a case like that? 'I'm so sorry,' she murmured at last, longing to comfort him but afraid of saying the wrong thing and making matters worse.

'So that's why I applied to come here, you see. I couldn't stay where there were so many memories, both good and bad. Some day I may go back, but not yet.'

The sound of the clock striking brought them back to the present moment.

'Good heavens, is that the time? I

must get going. My dog will think I'm never coming home. He'll be waiting to greet me when I arrive, desperate to get out for a walk.'

So that was where Richard disappeared to each lunchtime. There had been much conjecture about this, especially on the part of Lacey Drew, who obviously had her eye on the handsome young bank manager.

'Give him a pat from me.' Sophie smiled. 'I've always wanted a dog, but it's no good thinking about it while I'm living in a flat. Perhaps one of these days . . . '

'In the meantime, you might like to join us on one of our weekend walks. You'd love old Rex. He's nothing special as breeds go, a real Heinz 57 varieties, but he has a heart of gold.'

'I'd like that,' Sophie assured him, meaning it with all sincerity.

10

'That was Sophie,' Kate remarked, putting the phone down. 'She's on her way over here, so do you think you might, um . . .'

'Make myself scarce? I can do that very thing. I suppose she wants to discuss plans for her wedding, and I can do without all that talk of guest lists and flower arrangements.'

Kate hastened to interrupt before Mark had a chance to put two and two together and make five. 'Quite the opposite, I'm afraid. She didn't want to say too much over the phone, but it seems she's broken off her engagement with James. She'll need a bit of moral support now.'

'She's better off without that fool. Did you see the way he carried on last night? Not a thought for those poor souls at Rosebank, frantic with worry over losing their homes and their friends. Cosying up to Griff Hargreaves, and hanging on his every word. I could see by the look on her face that Sophie was mortified.'

Shortly after Mark had taken himself off to the pub, Sophie arrived, bearing a bag of cream cakes. 'Where's the coffee? I have a feeling this is going to be a long session, so I've come prepared.'

'Good. I can't wait to hear all your news.' Kate was truly sorry that her friend was going through a bad time, yet she had felt for a long while that James wasn't good enough for her. So how could she be anything but pleased that their engagement, if you could call it that, had fallen through?

'I gather you've had words,' she began, licking cream off her fingertips.

'It's finished, Kate.' Sophie seemed quite calm. In fact, Kate thought she could detect a steely resolve in her eyes. 'I won't get into all that's gone before; you know how many times I've had a good moan about James's shortcomings. But something happened today that made me realise we aren't right for each other. I happened to have a chat with Richard Kennedy after work, and he told me something about himself that started me thinking. Don't put this about, Kate; it's no secret, of course, but I don't suppose he'd wants it getting round the office.'

'You know I'd never repeat anything you tell me in confidence, but are you sure you should let me in on it?'

'Oh, it's not a scandal or anything. He was engaged to a girl who died of cancer. Naturally it hit him very hard. I could tell that he was deeply in love with her. He wanted to marry her despite everything, but she refused, saying she just wanted him to remember the good times.'

'Oh, Sophie!'

'That's how love should be, Kate. Two people wanting the best for each other. After Richard told me his story I realised that I just didn't love James enough, and it wasn't fair of me to marry him when my feelings weren't strong enough.'

'And not fair on you, either, with James being the man he is,' Kate mused, but she managed to keep that thought to herself. 'So that's what you told James?'

'Yes, and it wasn't very nice, I can tell you.'

Perhaps she had caught him at the wrong moment, but James had vented his spleen on her in no uncertain terms.

'I consider you've treated me very badly, Soph!'

'I don't think . . . '

'You've said your piece; now let me have my say! You've led me around by the nose for four years — four years! — and now you have the nerve to tell me it's all over? I've made you an honourable proposal of marriage and not only do you fling it in my face, but you keep me hanging about for days before you deign to give me an answer!'

'Steady on, James! Marriage is a

serious business. I felt I should think it over carefully before I agreed to enter into a commitment that should last the rest of our lives. It was only fair to both of us.'

'Fair! You call this fair! I know I'd make a pretty good husband, so what's your problem? I took you out for a nice meal, made my proposal in topnotch surroundings; isn't that what you women always say you want?'

'But you didn't say one word about love,' she countered miserably.

'Is that all that's bothering you? Just because I'm not the demonstrative type . . . '

'Words are important. You, of all people, should know that, since you expect to become a writer.'

It was the wrong thing to say. 'Now you're casting aspersions on my ability to write! I knew this had something to do with it! You were pleased enough to be with me when I was a high flyer in the public relations business, but now I'm taking off in a different direction you don't want to know, because you're convinced I'm about to fail as an author!'

This announcement was followed by much more in the same vein. As the succession of home truths came flooding out, Sophie sat with her head bowed, like a tree bending before the storm. There was a great deal she could have said but she pursed her lips tightly and clenched her fists inside the pockets of her jeans.

Mistaken though he was in his opinion of her, she couldn't blame James for being upset. After all, he was being dumped and that was never a pleasant experience for anyone. She was determined to get through this without saying things she'd regret later.

When at last he'd wound down and was sitting on the edge of the sofa with his head in his hands, she stood up to go. 'I can't tell you how sorry I am that things didn't work out between us,' she whispered, 'but I hope the time will come when you're able to agree that we're doing the right thing in breaking off before it's too late.'

'And that's where we left it,' Sophie told Kate now. 'Apart from James bawling after me to shut the door on my way out.'

'Well, if it had to come, at least you've got it over with. It can't have been very pleasant.'

'It certainly wasn't, and now it's done and reality is beginning to sink in, I'm feeling a bit lost. Sort of adrift, if you know what I mean.'

'Of course you are. After being part of a couple for four years it's bound to feel strange. If he comes begging you to go back to him, you'll have to make sure you don't get sucked back in. That's if a clean break is really what you want?'

'Yes, it is. It's quite a relief in a way. I can see now that my instincts have been pushing me towards this for some time, only I refused to listen.'

'What happens now, then?'

Sophie shrugged. 'The world is my

oyster, as they say. Now I'm free I can go anywhere, do anything. Ask for a transfer, change careers, go to Africa and nurse lepers. But how do I choose?'

Kate jumped up. 'Stay right there. Don't move a muscle until I get back.'

'What are you talking about?'

'Prunes!'

Puzzled, Sophie followed her friend into the kitchen. Kate produced a covered bowl and proceeded to tip the contents on to a plate.

'I was keeping these for breakfast, but never mind. I don't object to sacrificing them in a good cause!' she babbled. We had prunes and custard for our evening meal. At least, Mark did. I'm not overly fond of prunes, so I stewed a few figs and dried apricots as well. They don't have stones, of course.'

'Have you gone mad?'

'Certainly not. The thought just came to me. Cherries are not the only fruit with stones. We'll just see what these prunes have to say about your future.'

'You are an idiot, Kate Kent!' Sophie

was laughing now, and she entered into the spirit of the game by raking through the leftover fruit. 'Now that James is in the past I want to know who's next on the horizon. Tinker, tailor . . . '

They were laughing so hard that they didn't hear the door bell at first. Finally Kate roused herself and opened the door to find Griff Hargreaves standing on the mat.

'Don't tell me there's someone home after all! I thought I'd had a wasted journey.'

'Won't you come in?'

'Just for a moment. I can't stop long. I came to drop off some of these writing magazines for James Simpson. I imagine you'll see him one of these days, or your friend will.' He broke off as he noticed Sophie. 'Ah, good. I'll let you take charge of these, then, shall I? They're full of brilliant articles designed to help the novice writer.'

'I'm afraid I shan't be seeing James again,' Sophie said with dignity. 'We've come to a parting of the ways.'

'Have you? Ah well, easy come, easy go, as I always say.'

Kate winced as she sucked in a long breath. Talk about an insensitive remark! She glanced at Sophie, but Sophie didn't seem to mind.

'Better fish in the sea, Mr Hargreaves.'

'Exactly. Isn't it amazing how the old clichés always seem to fit the bill in times of trouble? Now you're on the loose, I don't suppose you'd care to trip the light fantastic with an aging author?'

'Thanks for the offer,' Sophie grinned, 'but I'm already taken. I'm going to marry a beggar man. I've read my fortune right here in these prune stones!'

★　★　★

'So I thought, we all thought, that Wednesday afternoon would be the best time to catch them.'

'Catch who, Mrs Philpotts? I didn't quite hear what you said.' Kate had been passing the scanner over the lady's books and hadn't been paying attention.

Mrs Philpotts glanced over her shoulder before hissing a reply out of the side of her mouth. 'The Carseleys, of course. Who else?'

'Oh, yes, I see.' Kate hid a smile. Other than the staff, and one man who was working his way through the rack of newspapers, there was nobody else in the library. There was really no need for this cloak and dagger stuff, although she did realise that Mrs Philpotts was a relic of the wartime days when posters all over Britain cautioned citizens that walls have ears.

The older woman looked at her with exasperation hidden all over her face. 'I don't think you do see, Miss Kent! I gather that nobody — the newspapers and our committee included — has been able to locate them to find out what's going on, and time is running out. Of course, they have never been about the place twenty four hours a day; the place runs quite nicely without them. Ever since the news came out, though, they seem to be even more elusive.'

'Mmm hmm.'

There was a pause. 'I'm not quite sure what it is you want me to do, Mrs Philpotts.'

'I want you to let that young man of yours know about Wednesday. It's Maisie Hammond's one hundredth birthday, and how she's going to have a happy one, not knowing where she might be this time next year, I really don't know! There's to be a big celebration in the common room at three o'clock, and the Carseleys have agreed to be there. If Mr Roberts can turn up, he might learn something to our advantage.'

Kate was pretty sure that Mark was meant to be working on that day, but she agreed to pass the message on. She doubted whether the couple would in fact make an appearance, but it seemed to be the only hope they had in catching up with them.

'I can't possibly get off on Wednesday,' Mark groaned, when Kate told him what Mrs Philpotts had said. 'I've switched shifts twice recently as it is, and I know that Staff Nurse Williams booked that day off ages ago, to go to her parents' ruby wedding, so she can't fill in for me. Somebody else will have to do it.'

But after making a few phone calls he came back into the living room, looking gloomy. 'Can you believe it? There's no one available. Nobody at all.'

'Surely there must be someone!'

'Nope! The colonel's buzzed off to France, and James Simpson seems to have fallen by the wayside. He was quite short with me and said he's got better things to do than running around following up lost causes.'

'I suppose he's out of sorts because of his break up with Sophie.'

'Maybe he is, but there's no need to take it out on me!'

'Have you tried Griff Hargreaves?'

'No joy there, either. He's off on some tour or other, promoting his new book. That only leaves the two women at Rosebank, but as they haven't managed to get the inside story by now, I'm sure they won't learn anything useful on Wednesday. Now, it needs an outsider to wheedle something out of the Carseleys.'

Kate went on polishing her brown leather pumps and she nearly jumped out of his skin when Mark pounded his fist on the table.

'I've got it! You can go in my place!'

'Oh, no, you don't! What on earth do you think I can do? I'm not even a member of the committee. And you're not the only one who's supposed to be on duty that day.'

'Ple-e-ease?' he begged, his eyes wide open and pleading.

'Oh, do get that sick puppy dog look off your face, Mark Roberts! If it means so much to you, I'll do it, but don't expect me to learn anything new. I'm not a private eye or a newspaper reporter.'

So on Wednesday afternoon she turned up at Rosebank, hoping to blend in with the expected crowd. The centenarian was sure to have an assortment of grandchildren and great grandchildren there, and with any luck Kate might be taken for one of them.

As it happened, there were very few outsiders there.

A man wearing a clerical collar was giving a little speech as Kate lingered in the doorway, but he waved her in and she was forced to take her place in a front row seat, where she felt most conspicuous.

'As I was saying, our dear sister was never blessed with children but here at Rosebank she is surrounded by friends who are as dear to her as any family could be.'

'And how long is that going to last?' a quavering voice demanded. All heads turned towards the speaker, a bent little man in a wheelchair. 'There's all this talk of closing us down, but will anyone give us a straight answer?'

'This is neither the time nor the place, Mr Rhodes,' a woman snapped. This was Mrs Carseley, of course. Kate remembered her now; she'd been at that initial protest meeting at the library, although she'd kept quiet while her husband had done the talking. There was no sign of Carseley himself today.

'It's about time somebody let us know what was going on!' Rhodes shouted. 'I'm not scared of you, madam! I fought against Hitler in the last war, I did, and lived to tell the tale! I reckon I can stand up to you just as well!' There was a smattering of applause at this.

He makes it sound as though he came face to face with Hitler in some sort of duel, Kate thought, but obviously his fellow residents appreciated the sentiment because they were still clapping.

'Oh, very well!' Mrs Carseley stepped forward, pulling her tunic down over her ample hips as she came. 'Do let's get this over with, so we can go back to the real purpose of this gathering. I don't know what more I can tell you.

'As I've said from the outset, much as we regret it, we have to give up because we simply cannot make ends meet. We feel sorry for you all, and we sincerely hope that you'll all find suitable accommodation in the near future, but you must see that we cannot keep throwing good money after bad.'

'So instead you've decided to make a fat profit by selling out to this development company we've read about in The Gazette,' Mrs Philpotts called out. 'A place this size, with acres and acres of land, must be worth millions. Who cares about a handful of old folks when you can get your hands on that kind of money? You're sacrificing us for thirty pieces of silver. That's what I call it!' She sank down on her chair, flushed and triumphant. This time the applause was louder and more prolonged.

Then came the bombshell. 'Oh no, Mrs Philpotts. You're quite wrong about that.'

Later, Kate reported back to Mark, who raised his eyebrows in amazement.

'I say! This is a turn up for the books! I wonder how The Gazette missed this one? So you're saying that the Carseleys don't own Rosebank after all?'

'Apparently not. They own the business, of course, but the actual building is only leased. That's why they can't do anything to stop the sale. Oh, they will get a modest pay out in return for allowing their lease to be broken, but that's a drop in the bucket compared with what the land is worth.'

'Then who does own the place? Did she say anything about that?'

Some old boy called Tony Lemming, or Lessing. I couldn't make that out. Apparently Rosebank was his family home, but that sort of place is far too big for one person nowadays. It was different when people had a dozen children and could afford to pay servants to do the work. Imagine the cost of keeping up a place like that now.'

'So leasing the place for a retirement home must have seemed like a good idea. It brought him a nice little income, and kept the place from going to wrack and ruin at the same time.'

'He was probably quite content to go along with that, until one day he realised how much the place was worth in terms of today's values.'

'So when he was approached by the development company Lessing, or whatever he calls himself, saw the chance to get rid of the white elephant and go off into the sunset to live happily ever after.'

'I suppose you can't blame him,' Kate sighed. 'It's all very well for us to say he should be a saint and give all he owns to the poor, or in this case, the soon to be homeless residents . . . '

'Not so poor if they can afford the pretty stiff fees the Carseleys charge,' Mark interrupted, but she shook her head crossly.

'That was a figure of speech. I was going to say that it's his property to sell, and for all we know he could be living in some grotty little flat, existing on a pension.'

'Hardly that, if he's been raking in a good income from the lease.'

'You know what I mean! If I had the chance of selling something which would give me an easier lifestyle as a result, I'm not so sure I'd pass it up, and neither would you, Mark Roberts!'

'That's a matter of opinion,' he responded, 'and it's hypothetical, anyway. We could argue about it till the cows come home, but the fact of the matter is, this has scuppered any chance of us saving Rose-bank. It's the end of the line, Kate.'

11

The girl held the phone tucked between her shoulder and her chin. By the look of her defeated expression she had some talkative customer on the line. She raised her eyebrows and pointed a finger towards the ceiling to indicate that she would only be a moment. The well dressed gentleman with the briefcase shifted his weight from one foot to the other.

'So sorry!' the girl said at last, replacing the phone in its cradle. 'As you may have gathered, that was a difficult customer. She called to complain because her paper hasn't been delivered, and she just won't accept the fact it's because her subscription has run out. Now, how can I help you?'

'I'd like to see the editor, please.'

'I'm sorry, that won't be possible today.'

'Why not? Isn't he here?'

'He's in the building, yes, but he can't see anyone. This is the day we put the paper to bed. He's doing a last minute check before the presses start to roll. He never sees anyone while that's going on.'

'I really think he'd want to see me!'

Biting her lip, the girl began to twist her hair around a finger. 'I'm sorry, I've got my orders. It's more than my life's worth to interrupt the editor at this stage. If you'd like to make an appointment he'll be pleased to see you another day, I'm sure.'

'And I feel sure that if you don't let him hear what I've got to say, before those presses start to roll, you'll be in trouble anyway. So trot along, please, and see what you can do.'

'I'll do my best, but I can't promise anything. What name shall I say?'

'Frederick Bolton, solicitor.'

The girl scuttled off. Moments later, the roar that could be heard throughout the building indicated that she hadn't exaggerated what the editor's reaction was likely to be. Bolton marched through into the workroom beyond, to be greeted by an enraged bull of a man.

'I think you should hear what I've come to say, sir! I'm a solicitor, representing Miss Jessie Golightly, part owner of Rosebank.'

'If you've come to complain about the stories we've been running, my reporter isn't here. In any case, I'm satisfied that he's conducted a careful investigation. We've printed nothing that can't stand up in court, so if your client is hoping to sue us, I'm afraid you've had a wasted journey. Good day to you, sir!'

'On the contrary, my client is most grateful to you for bringing this matter to light. Until she read the clippings of your articles, which someone was kind enough to forward to her in Bournemouth, she had no idea that the place had been put up for sale.'

'Part owner, you say? We understood that Mr Lessing was the sole owner.'

'That is not the case. When old Mr Norman Lessing died, Rosebank was left jointly to Miss Golightly and her cousin, Mr Tony Lessing. He'd had two children, who predeceased him. Mr Philip was killed during the Normandy landings at D Day, while his sister, Mrs Golightly's mother, died during the Blitz. The two cousins, his grandchildren, were Mr Norman's sole heirs.'

'And do you mean to tell me that the present Mr Lessing is deliberately trying to sell Rosebank behind his cousin's back?'

'It would seem so, although there is some thought that he may be, how shall I put it, becoming senile? Naturally Miss Golightly wants the sale to be stopped.'

'I see. This certainly puts a different complexion on things. So what is it you want us to do, Mr Bolton? You realise that we have to follow this story up? There's a great deal of bad feeling in the district over Rosebank's threatened closure, but I'm not sure that I want

The Gazette to become embroiled in family squabbles, unless it has a direct bearing on the matter.'

The solicitor scratched his ear, apparently trying to decide what he did want. The clock on the wall was ticking away madly and the editor glanced at his watch, rather pointedly. Mr Bolton grimaced.

'I'm not sure how far things have gone from Mr Lessing's point of view. That I have yet to determine. Has anything been signed? Has money changed hands? This is quite a tangled affair, I'm afraid, one that may take some time to unravel. I suppose I thought that if you were put in the picture it might prevent The Gazette from printing something, in all innocence, which could prove to be an embarrassment to you later.'

'Very good of you, I'm sure.'

'So perhaps you'd like to make mention of this new development in the forthcoming issue?'

The editor frowned. 'We'll certainly

follow this up, Mr Bolton, but saying anything in this week's paper would be premature. We'll have to speak to Miss Golightly first, of course.' He held up a warning hand as the little solicitor seemed about to protest. 'I don't doubt your word for a moment, but it's our business to cover all the angles. I'm sure you understand that.

'We'll need some inkling of what the outcome of all this may be. Does it give Rosebank a temporary reprieve, for example. I will make some slight changes to the story we're about to run this week so that word of our new discoveries, whatever they may be, will follow on smoothly in the coming weeks. Perhaps add a teaser, explaining that startling new developments will shortly be revealed.

'If you'd like to come this way I'll show you what's already in the pipeline and you can look over my shoulder while I make one or two changes.'

The next morning Chip McNaughton came in early. On publication day he liked to sit down with The Gazette and a cup of coffee and spend a quiet half hour reviewing his own input. He was still new enough at the job to take pleasure in gloating over the pieces he'd written, especially when he'd been awarded a byline.

Each article would be read over several times, while he congratulated himself on his fine writing, or winced over a word that had been repeated once too often. After that the pieces would be carefully clipped out of the paper and placed in his scrapbook. This wasn't just vanity, of course; he was busy compiling a portfolio of work which, he hoped, would help him land his next job. Onwards and upwards, that was Chip's motto.

His main effort this week was the continuing saga of the Rosebank closure. He was pleased to note that it had not yet been relegated to the inside pages, which was good. He read down the column with growing delight, and then his mouth dropped open with shock. What had happened to his carefully crafted ending? It had disappeared, and in its place was a short paragraph promising exciting developments to be reported next week!

What developments were these? Surely he hadn't written that! He sat back, feeling resentful. It was, of course, the editor's prerogative to make changes to the work handed in by the reporters but, dash it all, it was his story! Before he could think twice he jumped to his feet and ran into the editor's office.

He found the man leaning back in his swivel chair, with his feet up on the desk.

'Ah, there you are, Chip! Come in, my boy, come in! What do you think of the paper today, hey?'

'About my story,' Chip began.

'Ah, yes I was coming to that. There's been a development, and from our point of view it's a pretty good one. I had a visit from a solicitor yesterday, representing the owners of Rosebank, or at least one of them.'

'Don't tell me they want to sue,' Chip moaned. 'I've been extremely careful with this story, chief! Honestly, I can give you all my sources to back up what I've written!'

'Calm down, chum! There's nothing wrong with your work. You listen to what I've got to say, and you can take it from there.' He went on to explain what had been told to him the evening before.

'So you want me to track down this Miss Golightly and get her side of the story,' Chip said, his eyes sparkling.

'It'll need careful handling, mind. And I don't want a lot of unsubstantiated 'he said, she said' stuff. Then you can go and take a look at the old man's will. Check out the terms. See if it includes any provision for what's meant to happen if one party wants to sell and the other doesn't.'

'Does this mean that Rosebank gets to carry on if the lady refuses to sell?'

'That's what we need to find out. And another thing; what if she digs her heels in but the Carseleys are still determined to throw in the towel? A woman of her age is hardly likely to come down here to keep the place running herself, is she? No, one way or the other, Rosebank is still on the chopping block.'

Sophie was enjoying a walk in the country, glad to have left the bustle of the town behind her on this bright afternoon. It was surprising to discover that she now had so much time to spare for the things she really wanted to do. It felt strange to be on her own after four years of being part of a couple, yet it did have its advantages. Instead of obsessing over what might have been, she decided to indulge herself with outings that made her soul sing.

It was a shock to realise how much time she'd invested in making James happy at the expense of her own needs. Of course people in a relationship had to make an effort to share each other's interest and activities, but how far were you supposed to go with that? A spring came into her step as she strolled along, vowing that she had attended her last football game. Better yet, she would never again have to attend one of James's beastly office parties.

In fact, she might as well admit it, she wasn't the party type. Standing in a crowded room, shouting herself hoarse in an attempt to carry on a conversation over an unbearable level of noise, was not her cup of tea. Life was too short to waste it on activities you didn't enjoy.

'I'm going to pamper myself,' Sophie announced, to the amazement of a passing terrier, who stopped to sniff at her trouser leg. She laughed at herself. 'I must be going mad, talking out loud to myself like this.'

She leaned on a nearby field gate, continuing her train of thought. 'I'm going to have lovely evenings at home, watching soppy movies instead of thrillers, I'm going to catch up on my reading, and I'm certainly going to see more of Kate. Life is for living, and I'm going to make the most of it!'

'I couldn't agree more!'

She knew that voice, didn't
Embarrassed, she swung round to fac
Richard Kennedy, who was just dis-
mounting from a bicycle.

'I didn't hear you coming. I was
talking to the dog! There was one here a
minute ago, I assure you. Some sort of
terrier, it was.'

'I believe you; thousands wouldn't!'
he laughed. 'Actually, that was my old
Rex!' He looked quite different today;
more relaxed, even younger, if that were
possible. In the office he wore sober,
bank manager suits with quiet ties, but
today he was dressed in jeans and a
dark green fleece windbreaker, and an
American style cap with a long visor to
keep off the sun.

'It's nice to get out of town for a bit,'
Sophie murmured, suddenly feeling
shy. Normally it wasn't like her to be at
a loss for words, but somehow meeting
him here had caught her off balance.

'Yes, it is. I often wish I didn't have a
job that keeps me cooped up indoors all
day.'

'What would you rather do, then, if you didn't have a career in banking?'

Almost without realising it Sophie found herself continuing her walk, with Richard strolling alongside, wheeling his machine, and Rex panting along behind.

'Oh, when I was young I had dreams of working in forestry, or something like that, but Dad wanted me to follow in his footsteps. More money in that, he used to say, not to mention social cachet. According to him people will always need a place to store their valuables and to make financial transactions, so there will always be banks.'

'There'll always be trees, too,' Sophie pointed out, and they laughed gently.

'And you, Sophie? Is banking part of your dream?'

'I used to think it was. Oh, I meant to get married, and possibly produce the two children that James thought would be appropriate, but I expected to be able to continue my career in due course. Nowadays women do, don't they? Not just from choice, either. People with a mortgage need two salaries coming in. Now I'm not so sure if I want to keep number crunching for the rest of my life. It's not too late to change course if only I can decide what I'd like to do.'

'I rather hope you'll stay on at the bank for a while yet,' Richard said softly.

'Oh, don't worry. I won't leave you in the lurch. I'll make sure you know the ropes before I leave the branch.'

'That wasn't quite what I had in mind, Sophie.'

Her heart leapt. Was he trying to say he had feelings for her? And if he was, how did she feel about that possibility? She had just come out of a difficult relationship. It was too soon to get involved with somebody new. And yet . . .

Evidently her hesitation had transferred itself to him, for he did not go on to explain. Instead he made some remark about the lane they were

151

walking on, and asked if she knew where it led to.

'Oh, yes, of course.' She was relieved by the change of subject. 'I grew up round here, you know, so I know every inch of the place. As a teenager I couldn't wait to get away, and I did leave for a while, but then when I had the chance of a job here I jumped at it! You'll think I'm pretty silly, I suppose.'

'Not at all. And what about your old school friends? Have they moved on by now?'

'Most of them have, but luckily for me my best friend, Kate, has also returned to Branksome to work. She's head librarian, you know.'

'Isn't she the one who lives with Nurse Roberts, the chap who is involved with the Save Rosebank campaign?'

'The very one.'

They walked on without saying a word, but it was a companionable silence, not the difficult sort of quiet where you desperately tried to think of something interesting to say, yet manage to come up with nothing.

When they arrived at a crossroads Richard looked up and down, wondering which way to go. 'Where are we, then? You did say you know this district like the back of your hand.'

'Turn right and it takes you out to the main road. Turn left and it takes you up hill and down dale until eventually you arrive back in town. You choose, and please don't feel you have to stay with me. I'll be turning back soon. My feet are telling me I've gone far enough for one day.'

'Actually I was hoping we'd find somewhere to buy a drink. My tongue is sticking to the roof of my mouth.'

'You should have brought a bottle of water with you, then.'

Richard laughed. His face lit up in a way which altered his usual wistful expression, and Sophie found herself laughing in return.

'I could murder a glass of something cold,' he told her.

She decided to take pity on him. 'There's a pub about a mile down the road. We could call in there, if you like.'

'The very thing! Hop on behind me, then, and I'll give you a lift.'

'Richard, we can't! What if some earnest policeman comes along and stops us? How is it going to look if you finish up in court, charged with reckless biking, or whatever they call it? The Gazette will have a field day! Think of the headlines! Bank Manager caught wobbling on the public thoroughfare, aided and abetted by the Assistant Manager! We'd never live it down!'

'I dare you!' Richard said, his eyes twinkling.

'You're on!' Before she could stop herself she was perched on the seat of his bike with her legs dangling to the side. She had her arms around Richard, who was leaning on the handlebars, pedalling for all he was worth.

Laughing, they arrived at the White Goose, almost tumbling off the bike as they lurched into the cobbled yard.

'You order for both of us,' Sophie gasped. 'I must pop inside and tidy up. I can't think what I must look like!'

The mirror in the tiny loo reflected a red faced young woman with hair flying all over the place. That person looked a great deal happier than the rather sad girl who had looked back at her recently from the glass at home. The outing had done her good. Was doing her good, she corrected herself. It wasn't over yet.

'I have news!' Richard said, as she joined him at the table he'd chosen. 'In case you're wondering why we almost came to grief when we turned in here, it's because I've got a puncture in my back tyre.'

Sophie grinned. Nothing could dampen her happiness now. 'Then you'll have to mend it, won't you,' she instructed him.

'I would if I had a mending kit on board, but I don't. So I'm afraid we'll have to walk all the way back to town.'

'Well, Richard Kennedy, I hope you didn't expect I was going to ride on the back of your bike all the way home! It's one thing to play the fool out in the middle of nowhere, quite another to do it where we're sure to be seen!'

'In that case we'll have to walk back together,' he decreed, and Sophie found that she didn't mind the thought of that at all!

12

Chip McNaughton wondered if he'd come to the right place. The doors and window frames of the 1930s type villa looked to be in dire need of a coat of paint, and when he tried to ring the doorbell it came off in his hand. Perhaps Miss Jessie Golightly was down on her luck, and that was why she wasn't about to let her cousin do her out of the millions that were rightfully hers.

The elderly lady who answered the door looked genteel enough. Dressed in a tweed skirt and a hand knitted twin set, with a string of pearls around her neck, she appeared to be straight out of a black and white movie about the war years.

'Let me see your identification, young man. I'm not letting you over my doorstep until I'm satisfied you are who you say you are.'

Since he hadn't said a word so far this was a bit thick, and he had of course telephoned to say he was coming, but he meekly brought out his wallet and showed her his Gazette card with his photo on it. Nodding grimly, she stood aside to let him in.

'Now then, young man. This business about Rosebank. I take it you are the one who wrote up all this nonsense about poor old dears being put out in the street?'

'Er . . .'

'Never mind. I expect that cousin of mine tried to pull the wool over your eyes, just as he's tried it with me. And I do owe you a vote of thanks because if you hadn't written all this sob stuff my friend, Mary, wouldn't have clipped it out and sent it to me, and I hate to think what might have happened then.

'My solicitor tells me that Tony wouldn't have had a leg to stand on, but that's hardly the point. Once that sale had been rushed through it would take years of litigation to sort this mess out, and you know what that means! Any money I might have got would all be wiped out by legal fees.'

She opened a leather-bound photograph album and turned the pages until she found what she wanted. 'Here's a picture of Tony and myself on the sands at Brighton, the little weed.'

Chip peered at the faded black and white snapshot, which didn't tell him much. It showed a small girl, dressed in the sort of elasticated bathing suit which had been popular in the nineteen fifties, and a taller boy, wearing droopy trunks and brandishing a wooden spade.

'Very nice,' he muttered, not quite knowing what was expected of him.

'It wasn't nice at all,' she snapped. 'I hated every minute I had to spend with that boy, but my grandmother would insist on pushing us together. Poor little orphans should stick together; she used to say, although at that point each of us still had one parent on the scene. Tony had lost his father, of course, but Auntie Jean was still very much alive. Right after that photo was taken Tony deliberately smashed my sandcastle to pieces. What do you think of that?'

Privately Chip thought that anyone who was still fuming over a bit of childish horseplay after half a century was not right in the head, but he could hardly tell the woman to get a life. 'That wasn't very nice of him,' he said instead. After coming all this way to get his story he couldn't risk alienating her now.

'It certainly wasn't, and the little weasel hasn't changed. The older he got, the worse he became.'

'What did you think when Rosebank was left to the pair of you jointly?' Chip asked, hoping to bring the old lady to the point.

'Rosebank! Daft name! It was always Hamilton House in our day. That's what it was called when it was first built, and that's how it should have stayed, but those nursing home people changed it for some reason. Yes, it was left to us jointly, and don't think I didn't know what Grandfather was up to when he did that! Grandma always hoped Tony and I would marry each other, but I'd sooner marry the coal man than tie myself down to that twerp! As it is I've been forced to stay in touch with Tony all these years because we were joint owners of that white elephant.'

'Why didn't you sell the place, then? You could have gone your separate ways long ago.'

Miss Golightly sniffed loudly. 'At first it wasn't possible. Naturally my grand-father had no idea when he was going to die; in fact, the will was made soon after Uncle Philip was killed at the Normandy landings. He wanted to prevent the place from being sold over our heads, if he died while we were still young, and our inheritance squandered. He also had the old fashioned idea that I had to be protected from fortune hunters, men who tried to marry me just so they could get their hands on my money. He stipulated that the house could not be sold until I reached the age of thirty.'

'Which meant that Mr Lessing couldn't sell his share, either.'

'Exactly. Well, the house couldn't be left there to rot, so it was leased to a small private school for girls, and we received a small annual income as a result. Then the Carseleys came along and our money continued to trickle in. It isn't much, but when you're on a pension, every little helps.'

'I suppose so. Miss Golightly, what I'd really like to find out is what you plan to do now. Our readers will be interested to know, you see.'

She put up a hand as if she was a policeman, directing traffic.

'Much as I want to see Tony getting his comeuppance, I most certainly do not want our family disagreements splashed all over the newspapers!'

'Of course not, Miss Golightly.' Chip could just see his editor's face if he presented him with an article in which this feisty old lady was quoted as saying 'he stamped on my sandcastle so I'm getting my own back now.' He hid a smile.

'I'm more interested in the sale of Rosebank. Now you've got over the shock of your cousin's behaviour, I expect you'll be glad to sell your share to the developers, won't you? Think of it! No more worrying about stretching your pension to make ends meet.'

'My financial arrangements are no concern of yours, young man! But I do understand that these unfortunate residents of Rosebank, as you call it, will want to know what is going to happen to them. No, Mr McNaughton, I shall not be selling, and if my cousin, Tony, tried to take steps to force me into it, why, just let him try!'

'But why, Miss Golightly? Why won't you sell?'

'Taxation, young man! Oh, it may sound very nice on paper, my getting a half share of what the sale would bring, but the government will claw back much of that, one way or another. This way I shall still get my little dividend, so why should I kill the goose that lays the golden egg? After I'm gone Tony can do what he likes, but until then I'm in control of the situation, and that's that!'

'And that's the bottom line,' Chip told his editor when he returned to The Gazette office. 'It was like pulling teeth, but I finally got what I went for, and I'm quite sure the old girl won't change her position.'

'Interesting. I don't suppose you thought to call on Mr Lessing to get his side of the story?'

Chip shook his head. 'I did call at his house but there was nobody home. I spoke to a neighbour who told me he's gone away for a few days. Back next week, she thinks, because he's only asked her to feed his cat until Thursday. Mind you, I doubt if he'll have much to tell me when I do see him, other than presenting me with similar complaints about his childhood feuds with Cousin

Jessie. He wants to sell, and she doesn't, and never the twain shall meet.'

'Stalemate,' the editor pronounced. 'Nevertheless, we'll have to get his side of the story.'

'Of course,' Chip agreed, 'but what about the town council? Do you think they can force Miss Golightly to sell her share of the place?'

'Hardly. They have no reason, much less an excuse, to try to expropriate the property. It's not as if they want to push a road through the land or put up public buildings. This is an outside development company coming in with their eye on a good thing, and nothing at all to do with the town fathers.'

'As far as we know, chief! Someone could be taking backhanders, do you think? These developers have already offered a fat bribe to the Carseleys, to make them stand aside.'

'Hardly a bribe, Chip! An offer to buy them out, fair and square. It wouldn't hurt to nose around, though, just in case there's any corruption at the municipal level.'

Chip headed for his desk, aiming a kick at this inoffensive piece of furniture as he came. The Rosebank story showed all the signs of fizzling out like a damp squib. Hardly anything to write home about, and certainly nothing worth passing on to the big dailies. Fame and fortune would have to wait for another day.

In the meantime the next issue of The Gazette still had to be filled. Chip switched on his computer. It did not improve his mood when he found himself looking at a half-finished article on *Careers Day At The High School*. Boring!

Mark Roberts had been in a very strange mood ever since the news had broken that Rosebank was not to be sold. A final meeting of the Save Rosebank Committee had convened, but the future of the residence was still up in the air.

'It's very upsetting for everyone, not

knowing what's going to happen,' Mrs Philpotts reported. 'The Carseleys are still going to retire, so what's to become of us now?'

'They've announced their intention of selling the goodwill of their business,' the colonel pointed out. 'As I see it, we'll have to make a concerted effort to find new owners to take over.'

'And there should be some safe-guards in place,' Griff Hargreaves suggested. 'We don't want any old ragtag and bobtail coming along, thinking they can run Rosebank simply as a moneymaking business. They should have certain qualifications, or previous experience, don't you think?'

'I agree,' Mark put in. 'We certainly don't want to see an administrator coming in who'd have a view to the profit margin at the expense of the residents. It should be someone with a bit of money behind him, who can buy out the Carseleys without having a mountain of debt hanging over his head for the next ten years.'

'We can hardly enquire into a prospective buyer's finances,' the colonel reminded him, 'although naturally we shall require bank references and so on.'

'That's where I come in,' Richard Kennedy said. He had been invited to attend the meeting once the status of the Rosebank sale had been announced. 'I can advise on loans and mortgages, and I can do a background check on whoever shows an interest in taking Rosebank on. One can't be too careful these days, with all this talk of scams and identity theft.'

Standing in the doorway, waiting for the signal to bring in the tea tray, Kate watched Richard as he continued to talk about the possible pitfalls of bringing in outsiders without careful investigation. He seemed very nice, and, being a romantic at heart, she wondered what the chances were of something good happening between him and Sophie.

Sophie wasn't here tonight. She had

no reason to be, now that she and James were no longer an item. Come to that, James wasn't here, either. Kate suspected that he had lost interest now that he'd met Griff and squeezed what he'd wanted from that source. She meant to take Richard aside later and bring the conversation around to Sophie.

Dare she invite them both round for a meal? She didn't want to do anything to scare Richard away. Sophie had confided in her, telling her something about the man's background. While he seemed interested in her, it could be that he only wanted friendship, rather than romance.

'Because I know he's still grieving over the girl he was going to marry, Kate. I know he's lonely, and he doesn't know many people here yet. He knows me from work, of course, which is why we've got together a few times, just for a drink or a walk, not a proper date.'

'Surely it's more than that?' Kate smiled. 'You're not the only one he works with, and he hasn't asked any of them out, has he? Lacey Drew, for instance?'

'Lacey Drew! Give me a break! No, she's got her hooks into James now, believe it or not.'

'No! How did that come about?'

'She's met him in the past, when he used to come into the bank to speak to me, and I suppose she fancied him then. I gather she turned up at his flat one evening with a casserole and a bottle of plonk, and it went on from there.'

'You have to give her top marks for trying.'

'Yes, indeed, and she couldn't wait to drive the point home with me! She waltzed into the bank one morning and calmly announced that she and James were now an item. According to her she'd fancied him for a long time, but was too nice to make a move on him as long as we were together. Then when he dumped me — which is what she believes happened — there was nothing to hold her back.'

'Charming! I hope you told her where to get off!'

Sophie shrugged. 'I couldn't be bothered. James is free to date whomever he likes now, so I see no pointing letting the likes of Lacey Drew get to me.'

Now Kate thought she should help Sophie's new relationship along a little bit, but she didn't want to seem too pushy and perhaps ruin it. The fledgling relationship was still at the stage when any false move could drive a wedge between the pair. So what to do?

Richard and Mark seemed to be getting along well, so why not invite Richard round for a meal? And having done that, what would be more natural than for Kate to invite her own best friend to make up the numbers? They could prattle on about old times and Richard would never suspect Kate of having an ulterior motive.

She came back to the present with a start. Richard had completed his little speech now and it was Griff's turn.

'Are we all agreed that it's time to advertise for new people to operate Rosebank? If you wish, I'd be pleased to draw something up for your approval, now that the Public Relations expert is no longer with us.'

'As long as we run it by the Carseleys first,' the colonel remarked. 'Just to make sure that they are really leaving after all. And if they intend to sell the good will of the place we'll need to know their asking price. Not that we want to mention that in the advertisement, of course.'

'There is another way to go,' Mark broke in, his expression serious. 'Something we should consider before we go that far. We — this committee, that is — could form a board of directors to run Rosebank. How about that?'

'And bring in someone we'd pay to run the place on our behalf, you mean?' The colonel looked interested, but seated side by side on the settee the two ladies from Rosebank were fluttering like autumn leaves in a strong wind.

Little Miss Robson glanced at her companion with a look of horror on her face.

'Speaking for myself, I don't think I want to get involved in anything like that, not at my time of life,' Mrs Philpotts said firmly. 'And I certainly don't think that Flora is up to it. I don't mean any disrespect to you, Flora dear, but you know what your blood pressure is like. The doctor has insisted that you stay calm, and I feel sure that being made partly responsible for a place like Rosebank could put you under a great deal of stress.'

Miss Robson nodded, speechless.

'That still leaves three of us,' Mark insisted.

'It's worth some thought,' the colonel said, taking a quick look at his watch, 'but time is getting on and this is not a decision that should be rushed into. I suggest we go away to give it careful thought, and reconvene at the same time next week. Will someone make a motion to adjourn? Who seconds the motion? Right. Meeting closed.'

Kate was able to speak to Richard while he stood in the middle of the carpet, patiently waiting to leave. The Rosebank ladies were blocking the door as they twittered nervously to Colonel Browning about this new turn of events.

'I wondered if you'd care to join us for a meal one evening next week, Richard? You and Mark seem to have plenty in common, and I'm sure he'll be able to introduce you to other people you might want to get to know.'

'I'd be delighted. What did you have in mind?'

Later, when she told Mark what she'd done, he appeared vague. 'Sure, fine. Whatever you want. Just let me know what you're cooking and I'll pick up a bottle of wine on the way home.'

'And I'm going to invite Sophie, as well.'

'Why not?' He didn't seem to make the connection, which perhaps was just as well. Kate didn't need to be told that matchmakers can cause trouble, more often than not. It was worrying, though, that his vague air persisted over the next couple of days. When she couldn't stand it any longer she decided to tackle him about it.

'Something on your mind, Mark?'

'Huh? What do you mean?'

'It's just that you've been off in the clouds somewhere lately. There's not something wrong at work, is there?'

He hesitated, and then it all came pouring out. 'It's Rosebank, Kate. I've come to a decision. I'm going to buy into it and run it myself.'

'What?' she squeaked.

'Don't you see, it's tailor made for me! I'm a nurse, with additional geriatric qualifications, and I'm very much on the side of these people who stand to lose the roof over their heads and be shipped off to goodness knows where. I've been over to take another look at the place, and there's a lovely little flat on the top floor which would suit me down to the ground.'

'You mean you'll be leaving here, moving out?' Kate could hardly believe her ears.

'Well, yes. What's the point in paying rent when a flat comes with the job?'

13

Blinking back the tears which threatened to overwhelm her, Kate struggled to maintain her composure. She'd fretted for some time over the possibility of Mark leaving her, but she hadn't expected the end to come so abruptly. She wanted ·to scream and throw things, but if she was to have any chance of saving the situation she had to keep quiet. She gulped.

'And you didn't think to discuss this with me, Mark?'

'Actually, no. At first I wasn't even sure if it was what I really wanted to do, and then I had to look at the financial aspects. There was no point in bringing you into it until I had a clearer picture.'

'And is that picture clear to you now?'

'I think so. Yes.'

'Then when did you intend to tell

me?' Kate demanded, mentally stamping her foot.

He frowned. 'Give me a chance, will you? I've only just decided. I would have told you this evening only you stampeded me into this conversation first.'

Stampeded, was it! It made her sound like some nagging wife. This was her life, too! And surely, if Mark had come to the end of the road as far as their relationship was concerned, he could have wrapped up the news more gently? Again she reminded herself that a shouting match was no way to go.

'I don't understand where you plan to get the money for this,' she murmured. Perhaps she could persuade him that his Rosebank scheme was an impractical idea. Then he might stay on at the flat with her for a while, giving her the opportunity to win him back.

'Do you realise that that pretty little house on Morley Street sold for two hundred thousand the other day? A modest place like that? What on earth do you think a place like Rosebank would cost? Millions, I expect. How could you even come up with a down payment, let alone handle a mortgage, even supposing you could get one?'

'Oh, I'm not thinking of buying the property, you silly girl. Just the business, from the Carseleys. I bumped into Chip McNaughton on the way home, and he says that this business between the heirs to the place is all straightened out. There will be an announcement in the newspaper next week. Miss Golightly has flatly refused to have anything to do with the sale and her cousin has had to back down. No doubt the developers will come out fighting, but they're definitely out of luck, and, as nothing was signed, they can't even sue for breach of contract.'

'I see.'

'Come on, Kate! I expected you to show a bit more enthusiasm than this.'

'Did you!'

'I suppose this has come as a shock, has it?'

How could he not see that he'd just managed to knock all the stuffing out of her? Into the silence he said 'I expect you just need time to think about it. You'll soon get used to the idea. When we're both off duty at the same time I'll take you over to take a look at the flat. You'll love living there, Kate. It's twice the size of this one.'

Relief flooded over her. She wasn't being dumped after all! A minute later this was replaced by a tide of resentment. How dare he make this decision without consulting her! As for loving the new flat, well, she loved their present home, too. It was in a quiet neighbourhood in a pleasant area, only a mile from the library.

Except in the worst of weather she was able to walk to work. And how would she take to living in a residence for senior citizens? Not that she had anything against older people; far from it. At least they knew how to behave properly, unlike some of the younger people who frequented the library. It was the thought of living in a closed community again, like being back in a college dorm, or — or — like nuns in a convent! As for Mark, as the head man, (what was the male equivalent of being called Matron?) he would be on call around the clock. People would be tapping on their door at all hours.

He was regarding her anxiously. 'Are you worried about getting to work from there, Kate? I've checked it out. There's a good bus service and the number eleven stops right outside the library. And when you've had time to consider all the other good things about life at Rosebank you'll see what a great opportunity this is.'

'Such as?' she asked coldly.

'Well, meals, for one thing. They provide excellent meals at Rosebank, and we can either eat in the dining room or have meals sent up to the flat. It'll be like living in a luxury hotel. Wouldn't you like to come home from work without having to worry about shopping for the evening meal?'

Luxury hotel, indeed! She had no doubt that Rosebank was superior to many such places, but let's face it, institutional food was just that. Cooking for large numbers affected the quality, somehow.

'And then we'd have those lovely grounds to walk in,' he coaxed. 'You could get a dog, Kate. You've always wanted one but we decided it wasn't fair to leave an animal shut up in the flat all day. Now we'll get a nice, friendly animal who can have the run of the place. The residents will love it! So many of them used to have pets of their own, and having to give that up is one of the hardships of retirement living.'

This was all very tempting, but Kate knew she mustn't rush into anything. Her future was at stake as well.

'I can't make up my mind,' she said at last. 'It sounds as if you'll be set for life, but what about me? If we should ever break up, I'll have to be the one to leave. I won't even be entitled to part of our household assets, because everything will be part and parcel of Rosebank. You'll be sitting pretty and I'll be left with nothing.' Now the tears were unstoppable and she fumbled for her handkerchief, not caring if he did see how desperate she was.

Mark looked at her in amazement. 'What on earth is the matter, darling? Of course you'll never be in that situation!' He took her in his arms and she put her head on his shoulder, still sniffling. 'Listen to me, Kate!'

He moved back, holding her at arm's length. 'This isn't at all how I meant it to be. I was going to take you out, treat you to a slap up meal with all the trimmings, and then ask you to marry me. We can still have the meal, of course, but may I have my answer now? I do love you, Kate Kent! Will you marry me?'

'Do you mean it?' she sobbed, dabbing at her streaming eyes. 'You're not just saying it because I'm upset, are you?'

'How could you think that? I've seen what happened to James Simpson, losing Sophie because he's such a self centred fool. I want you at my side for the rest of our lives, Kate, so please don't keep me waiting any longer!'

'If you love me that much you have a funny way of showing it, Mark Roberts!' She was determined to milk the last drop of remorse out of him, but she was laughing as she said it. 'I suppose I'll have to marry you, if you feel that strongly about it.'

He gave a whoop of delight as he pulled her closer into his arms. There was silence for a long while as they sealed their bargain with a kiss.

THE END

FALSE PRETENCES

Phyllis Humphrey

When Ginger Maddox, a San Francisco stock-broker, meets handsome Neil Cameron, she becomes attracted to him. But then mysterious things begin to happen, involving Neil's aunts. After a romantic weekend with Neil, Ginger overhears a telephone conversation confirming her growing suspicions that he's involved in illegal trading. She's devastated, fearing that this could end their relationship. But it's the elderly aunts who help show the young people that love will find a way.